Praise for Andrea Dale

"Legendary erotica heavy-hitter."
—the über-legendary Violet Blue

"Incredibly erotic."
—Erotica-Readers.com

["The Queen of Christmas" is] "as perfect a blend of sex and humor as rum-spiked eggnog."
—Donna George Storey,
author of *Amorous Woman*

"'Fanning the Flames' by Andrea Dale is perfect for spanking fans and features a delicious twist."
—*Scarlet* magazine UK

["A Few Things to Pick Up on Your Way Home" is] "a sensual trip through humiliation and desire."
—Editor Shanna Germain

["Party Favor" is] "sharp, short, effective."
—Steve Isaak,
Reading & Writing by Pub Light

"'How the Little Mermaid Got Her Tail Back'" (in a sushi restaurant!) is as beguiling as a siren."
—Erin O'Riordan,
Urban Fantasy Writers

Also by Andrea Dale

Novels

A Little Night Music

Novellas

Braceleted
In Her Hands
Kiss on Her List

Collections

Give In
Kiss Me Hello
Naughty in Nature

quick LICKS

Sexy Nibbles and Hot Bites

ANDREA DALE

SOUL'S
ROAD
PRESS

Quick Licks
Sexy Nibbles and Hot Bites
Andrea Dale

Print edition published 2016 by Soul's Road Press

First Edition
ISBN-13: 978-1-946462-00-8

Inquiries should be addressed to
Soul's Road Press
info@soulsroadpress.com
http://www.soulsroadpress.com

Cover image © luckybusiness | Dreamstime
Logo designed by Designs by Trapdoor

Table of Contents

quick
LICKS

Sexy Nibbles and Hot Bites

lie back...

MY HAND WANDERS lazily to my cleft as I dream of green pastures and ancient, magic woods. Of castles and hill forts and Roman roads. Of cathedrals and holy wells.

My fingers flash over my clit as I taste leek pie and chips soaked in vinegar; smell curry and moss and legends.

I'm aching with need, desperate for release. Knights in armor, damsels in distress parade before me. I reach for my vibrator, turn it to high.

My back arches as I shudder and come to the tune of "God Save the Queen."

Sated, I lie back and think of England.

undoing the laces

I HADN'T REALLY wanted to go camping. I never do. I'm less of a roughing-it type and more of a room-service type. But my husband and I do historic re-enactment—dressing up in medieval clothes and hitting each other with sticks—so camping is a necessary evil.

By the end of this particular weekend, though, I had to re-think my position on the issue.

Because we haven't splurged on the big period pavilion, Greg and I are usually relegated to the "slums" on the outskirts of the encampment with the other modern tents. Which is fine. Our cabin tent is easy to put up and take down, which means we can throw our stuff inside, change into garb, and get down to having fun.

Plus, summer was lazing into autumn, and there wouldn't be many more perfect weekends with brilliant, clear blue skies and mellow temperatures.

We'd joined the period dance revel on the second evening, then done the rounds of the various camp-side parties. Thirsty from the whirling and spinning, I'd indulged in more homemade mead than I usually do. Which was why I was finding my way to the nearest porta-potty several hours after most everyone else had tamped down their fires and crawled into their sleeping bags. Oh, I could still hear some drumming and laughter in the distance, but those were the real die-hards.

I wasn't drunk, just pleasantly tipsy as I finished my business. My eyes had adjusted to the darkness, so I didn't bother to turn on my flashlight to go back to our tent. Of course, that meant I had to walk with more care, so I didn't step on someone's armor that had been left out to air or trip over a tent rope.

Which may be why I noticed the light in our friends Kelly and Brad's tent, which was pitched next to ours.

I was pretty sure they'd just gotten back from their own evening of carousing. I opened my mouth to make some comment about their partying ways when I heard something.

Kelly's low, breathy moan.

The sound throbbed straight into my clit. My belly contracted. It was the most erotic thing I'd ever heard. (Porn was fine for porn's sake, but there's nothing sillier than all those fake moans and groans, especially when they happen while the actress' mouth is full of cock.)

This was real. An honest sound of blatant passion.

Holding my breath, I eased open the zipper to our tent, one tooth at a time, and crept inside, repeating the careful process to close the flap behind me. The nylon of the tent crackled as I slipped back into the double sleeping bag on the air mattress.

"Did you hear something?" Kelly asked, sounding vague and distracted.

"Nah. Everyone's asleep," Brad whispered back. "No, leave the light on."

"Won't somebody see?"

"They're all asleep," Brad repeated. "And I want to see you." His voice was rough with lust.

Although I'd never thought of myself as a voyeur, right now I wanted to see, too. On my knees, I peered out the half-moon window in the side of our tent, which we'd unzipped to let in the soft night air and the comforting scent of wood smoke. I could see easily through the screening.

With the light on in their tent, I couldn't so much see Brad and Kelly as I could their silhouettes. Again, somehow it was sexier than seeing their fully naked forms.

Her head was tilted back, and he was kissing her throat, his mouth moving languidly down the slender column to the curve of her breasts. From her shape, I could tell she was still wearing her corset. The outline of a crumpled heap in the corner must have been her dress, carelessly tossed aside when passion took over for common sense and care for the handmade garment.

My breasts felt heavy. I brushed my hand across them. My nipples were hard beneath my linen nightdress.

I eased down into the sleeping bag, reached inside. Greg was wearing just a pair of thin drawstring pants. I cupped my palm around his flaccid cock through the linen and, as quietly as I could, whispered for him to wake up.

I had no idea whether it was my hand or my voice that actually woke him. I didn't really care, as long as he could share this with me.

He started to speak, but I shushed him, barely breathing as I told him to sit up and look.

"Holy… Brad and Kelly?"

I nodded.

"We probably shouldn't watch," I whispered. "But…I want to…"

At first Greg didn't say anything. Then, "Tell me why."

I squirmed inwardly; I wasn't always comfortable talking about how I felt in bed. But right now I was too horny to care.

"It's hot," I said honestly. "It's turning me on." To punctuate his words, I took his hand and showed him how my nipples were trying to poke holes through the weave of my nightdress.

I heard his sharp intake of breath. In the darkness, his eyes were like black pools of desire.

In the other tent, Kelly shifted position, kneeling facing away from Brad. Her head was bowed slightly, and I understood a moment why when Brad lifted her thick hair and commenced nibbling at the back of her neck.

I heard long exhalation, her almost indistinct "Mmm, yes."

My skin tingled in empathy. "Yes," I echoed.

Beside me, Greg slid his hand up my back to the nape of my neck. My hair was in a pair of braids, leaving the sensitive area exposed. I shivered as he trailed his fingers across my flesh. I would have loved to feel his mouth there, but I knew he wanted to watch, too.

That aroused me even more.

Now Brad began to unlace Kelly's corset. He didn't rush, pulling the long laces through the eyelets with excruciating slowness. As each inch of flesh was exposed, he bent and pressed his lips there, making a ritual out of the undressing.

Unbearably erotic.

As the corset fell free and the silk chemise beneath slid down, Kelly's breasts tumbled out, unrestrained. Kelly reached up, cupping her heavy mounds in her hands. She circled her nipples with her fingers, and I heard her whimper with pleasure.

"Do that," Greg said.

I stripped my now-confining nightdress over my head, caressed my own breasts. Not as large as Kelly's, but ample enough, and my nipples were delightfully sensitive.

Which Greg knew. "Pinch them," he said.

I couldn't see distinctly what Kelly was doing, but I could extrapolate. Hell, by this point, I didn't entirely care what exactly Kelly was doing. It was amazingly hot to watch, but I was desperate to feel, too.

My nipples sent electric signals to my clit, and as I played with myself, my hips pumped gently, moving to the primal rhythm of my fingers and my blood. Pleasure, a hint of pain, a throb of sensation.

Greg grazed his teeth across my bare shoulder, watching me, watching Kelly and Brad. My pussy felt swollen, slick.

Needy.

I abandoned my nipple and reached down, but Greg caught my wrist, guiding my hand to his crotch. He was rock hard, and he hissed between his teeth when I curled my fingers around him. I let go long enough to pull the drawstring bow free, then snaked my hand inside his pants to stroke him freely. Hot flesh, steely length. I couldn't remember the last time he'd been so hard. My thumb slipped through the bead of precome at his tip.

I brought my hand to my mouth to taste it, rubbing the sweetness against my lower lip.

For a moment it seemed as though the tables had turned, as if Kelly and Brad were somehow channeling us. Kelly turned, and I saw that I'd missed Brad stripping out of his pants—or maybe he hadn't been wearing them all along, and only now he'd turned to full profile and I could see his cock jutting up.

Kelly turned, and bent to take the proud length of him in her mouth.

My hand went back to Greg, and he clenched his fist around mine. Too much sensation; he didn't want to come, not just yet.

Neither, it seemed, did Brad. He pulled Kelly up, caressing her shoulders, her breasts, sliding his hands down into the indistinct area between them. Kelly squealed under her breath. My pussy clenched, wanting that.

A fumble of movement in the other tent, but clear enough to us. Brad sat facing Kelly, and she straddled him, sinking down on him while he nuzzled her breasts. He leaned back on his hands, and she rocked back and forth on him. He had a great view.

So did we.

Greg shifted behind me. He was on his knees, and he drew me back towards his lap. I spread my legs, straddling him as well, only backwards. Our knees would no doubt regret this in the morning, but right now, we didn't care.

All I cared about, certainly, was the feel of the length of Greg's cock sliding up inside of me. I bit my lip to keep myself from making too much noise. God, he felt so good inside me, filling me.

We couldn't really move much, not if we didn't want to be overheard. I suspected Kelly and Brad were so intent on their own rutting that they wouldn't have heard a phalanx of Roman guards rattle by, but I didn't want to take that chance, and neither did Greg.

Kelly's thrusts grew erratic. Greg, watching over my shoulder, reached around me to stroke his fingers against my clit.

Kelly had been whimpering, deep in her throat, as she obviously tried to keep quiet. Now the sound changed to a squeal. She clutched Brad's shoulders—I imagined her nails were digging into his back—as the sound rose in pitch.

The sights, the sounds, the feel of Greg's cock inside me and his fingers expertly teasing my clit, all sent me over the edge.

I stuffed my fist in my mouth to keep myself from screaming.

Distantly, I was aware of Brad hoarsely swearing and telling Kelly how much he loved her.

Greg jerked only once, twice. I clenched around him as he pulsed, my orgasm triggering his.

Kelly and Brad's orgasms triggering ours.

*

The next morning, as we were packing up our cars, I swear I saw Brad wink at Greg.

Yep, I might need to re-think my reluctance about camping.

the heist

"ON THE GROUND! Now!"

The harsh words echoed through the bank lobby.

Leroy ducked back into the hallway, praying he hadn't been seen. Granger's Bank had never in its fifty years been robbed, and now, two weeks after he'd taken the security guard job, it had to happen.

Just his luck.

He peered around the corner, holding his breath. Two of them, wearing nondescript dark clothes and stockings to mask their faces.

He eased back, considering his options.

"Put all the cash in this bag."

His bowels turned to ice.

Sherri. God, how he missed her smoky voice. Despite himself, his cock stirred.

"Check the vault."

Fuck. He knew that voice, too: Tom, the bastard Sherri had run off with.

Well, he wouldn't have a problem nailing Tom in the head with a bullet, but Sherri was another matter.

Leroy's gun slipped from his shaking hand. The sound of it hitting the marble floor was like a gunshot in itself, ricocheting around the corridor. Of course he panicked. He never thought he'd be a good security guard.

"What the hell?" Tom yelled.

"I'll take care of it," Sherri shouted back to him. She came around the corner with the shotgun cocked and ready to fire. His gun had skidded too far away. Leroy raised his hands and prayed.

"Well, fancy meeting you here." Sherri's features were smashed beneath the stocking, her curves lost beneath the baggy outfit, but her voice and her musky perfume were enough to make Leroy harder than the marble floor.

"Pick up that chair," she said, gesturing with her gun to a wooden straight chair in the hall. "Now get into the vault."

The damn thing was never locked during the day. Old Man Granger was that secure. He probably deserved to be robbed, filthy rich as he was.

Sherri hauled the massive door shut behind them. She used his own cuffs to secure one of his hands to the chair, then tied the other back with the partner to the stocking over her head.

"Don't make a sound," she said.

Helpless, he watched her shove bundles of cash into two canvas bags. When they were full, she cinched them up. But before she hauled them onto her back, she turned and regarded him.

"You are a sight," she said, shaking her head. "Seeing you trussed up is giving me bad ideas."

He tried to respond, but his mouth had gone dry.

Sherri cupped his crotch, laughed when she felt his unflagging erection and heard him suck in his breath. "Ah, what the hell."

She pulled up her blue denim shirt to reveal her braless breasts, nipples already puckered, the color of ripe plums. She fed him one, and he suckled eagerly. God, he'd missed her.

She stripped off one leg of her cargo pants and panties. The scent of her cunt made him twitch harder. He jerked against his bonds. He wanted to bury his face in her, then throw her down and plunge into her, make her scream his name.

With deft fingers she undid his polyester uniform pants. He lifted his ass so she could pull them and his boxers down. His cock sprang free, red and stiff. A drop of fluid at the tip glistened under the harsh fluorescent light. His balled ached with need.

Throwing one leg across his lap, she rubbed the head of his cock against her slick lips. "No time for teasing," she said, her voice a little hoarse. "There's a pity."

She sank down on him, her warm pussy surrounding him, pulsing along the length of him. She posted up and down, grinding herself against his cock. Her breasts bounced in front of his face and he tried to capture one with his mouth again.

He'd never known her to be so aggressive. Oh, she'd always been an enthusiastic lover, but this went beyond an uninhibited roll in the hay. And as much as he wanted his hands free—as much as he pulled at the restraints until his cuffed wrist ached—there was something about being held down that was pretty damn sexy. There was something about her taking the lead, something about her having all the control, that brought him to the edge faster than he'd ever gotten before.

He gritted his teeth as his balls tightened. Okay, it was a matter of pride, but not until she...

Fuck. He couldn't take it anymore. He thrust up hard into her—as best he could under the circumstances—and felt her spasm, shuddering through her own release as he came. She whimpered, bit his neck to keep herself from screaming.

She had the decency to pull his pants up over his sticky, spent cock. As if suddenly seized by a fit of tenderness, she pulled the stocking on her head up and kissed him, full and hard, before grabbing the bags and her gun and running out. Her footsteps receded down the hall, leaving him alone with the sound of his own harsh breathing and the mingled scent of their fucking.

Leroy twisted his wrist. All the jerking and pulling during their sex had loosened the stocking that bound him to the chair, and in a few moments, he was free.

He spit out the key she'd passed him in the kiss and went to work unlocking his other wrist from the cuffs.

He'd give his police report (nobody would be surprised that he'd screwed up; in fact, they'd expected it), get in his truck, and meet Sherri at the dam. They'd get rid of Tom—the reservoir was deep, and it was a long way down—and then they'd head downstate as planned.

And when they stopped at a motel, he was going to cuff *her* to the bed and see how much *she* liked the teasing….

the last rays
of the summer sun

IT WAS ANGEL'S turn to do the supper dishes.

Up until last month, dish duty had been shared by our twins, Kelly and Jacob. But with both of them now off to college, we were back to Angel and I trading off.

Strange, the little things that change when your kids leave home.

The dishes had actually piled up for a few days before we remembered to negotiate the chore, along with a few others left in the twins' wake. We'd also had to get used to the silence: no more of Kelly and Jacob's voices, music, footfalls down the stairs, or impassioned cell phone conversations.

Then again, there had been a few positive changes, too.

We'd replaced the silence with our favorite '80s tunes, breaking into spontaneous dance or song with no child to roll his or her eyes.

We'd also slowly defaulted back to our pre-kid clothing choices, or near-lack thereof. In the annual Southern California autumn heat wave, I was wearing a gray cotton sports bra and a pair of loose running shorts, and admiring the way the evening sun shone through Angel's thin sundress.

She wasn't wearing anything underneath it.

It was a cliché, but I'd always thought my Angel looked like her namesake, her red-gold hair now burnished by the setting sun, her curvy hips and thighs outlined beneath her sheer skirt.

As quickly as that thought entered my mind, another one chased it away: Fallen angel, more like it. She'd always been a delicious mix of curious and inventive in bed (and out of it), and a slow warmth pooled in my groin as the clock in the entryway chimed 7 p.m. and I remembered something I'd almost forgotten.

But before I could say anything, Angel wiped her hands on a cobalt-and-white checked dish towel, turned to me, and said, "Time for *Jeopardy!*"

And from the wicked glint in her brown eyes, I knew we were having the same thought.

Once the twins were old enough to have a bedtime past 7 p.m., Angel and I stopped playing our *Jeopardy* sex game. When they were old enough to enjoy the game show, we invented a chores version of the game, but by high school and various after-school activities on top of homework, they'd moved on, and Angel and I had never really picked it up again, spending our evenings with e-mail and whatnot before kicking back with a police drama or sitcom.

You do the math. It had been a long time.

My body, though, hadn't forgotten. My bra felt suddenly tight as my breasts swelled, my nipples peaking. Eager, hopeful…time to play?

I grabbed the remote, found the channel, as Angel came in from the kitchen. "Strip, baby," she said.

"Race you," I countered. "Before the credits are over."

The theme song sent a second frisson of heat zinging at my pussy. The race wasn't really fair: all Angel had to do was pop the bow at the back of her neck and tug her sundress off, so she was naked when I'd just barely gotten my damn bra unhooked.

"Penalty to Team Marisol!" She laughed and dropped onto the sofa next to me.

I didn't even think about protesting that we hadn't discussed ground rules. After all, I'd suggested the strip race... knowing I'd lose.

The rules had always been a bit fluid anyway. Whomever answered the question first, before both the other person and the TV contestant, won a point. If one of us answered the question first but incorrectly, though, that person received a penalty.

There were other rules, of course, for Daily Doubles and Final Jeopardy and whatnot, but that was the gist of it.

The rewards and penalties, of course, depended on our whims....

When we'd started, it actually hadn't been sexual. More like who had to do dishes, or one of us giving the other a foot rub. That hadn't lasted long, though. We were young, in love, and very, very frisky.

Now, she immediately demanded one of those foot rubs as my penalty. I dug my thumbs gently into the balls of her feet as she wiggled her toes with delight. Alex Trebek introduced the contestants, then the categories, explaining the rules we knew by heart.

When you've been with someone a long time, you kind of stop looking at them. Or, maybe it's that you stop seeing them. If you blindfolded me, I could describe every curve of Angel's body, every line, every mole; the spots that were ticklish, the areas that were always warm or always cool; the way she smelled, the breathy hitch in her voice when she was aroused.

But when was the last time I'd actually *looked*?

It felt ('80s cliché warning) like the first time.

I was utterly charmed and fascinated by the tiny furrow between her brows as she considered a question. I fell besotted and breathless once again with the curve of her collarbone, the dusky hardness of her nipples, the rounded pooch of her belly, the softness of her inner arm as I stroked it with my fingertips.

I felt dizzy with desire in a way I'd forgotten, and hadn't realized I'd forgotten until now.

Desire is fucking distracting, too, so I was missing questions left and right.

"What's up with you tonight?" Angel asked at the first commercial break.

"Just…distracted," I said. I started to explain, then stopped. How to put it into words? Instead, I abandoned her foot and slowly slid one hand up her smooth calf.

She caught her breath, her eyes fluttering shut for a moment. She shifted on the sofa, and I caught a whiff of her special scent, spicy and *her*. In echoing response, my own pussy flooded with moisture. I rose to my knees and leaned over her for a kiss, cupping her breast in my hand and feeling her nipple stiffen into my palm.

I was intent on her pleasure, which certainly brought *me* pleasure, but perhaps not quite as intensely. The way I figured it, I probably owed her due to my muffing so many questions. I swear I didn't have an ulterior motive.

I swear it didn't occur to me until the next round started, and Angel's brain was so lust-fogged that *she* screwed up several questions in a row, all in American History, a category she knew well.

Maybe if I kept distracting her….

Of course, Angel was sharp as a tack—one of the things I adore about her—and soon she was on to my trick. Things promptly dissolved into each of trying to distract the other through carnal shenanigans. While still trying to answer questions.

My mouth on her breast, I mumbled "What is MARTA?"

Her teeth gently tugging at my earlobe, she murmured "Who is Styx?"

My thigh between hers, bearing down, I crooned "What is *The Scarlet Pimpernel*?"

Her fingernails grazing my back, she gasped "What is the Waldorf Astoria?"

We were neck-and-neck (as near as I could keep count, which wasn't very much) when we rolled into Final Jeopardy. The category was Authors. This was my forté. I was golden. I moaned that I'd bet it all. That was my mistake.

Before the commercial break was over, Angel somehow had me pinned down, her three fingers crooked inside me, beckoning me closer and closer to orgasm.

Alex Trebek said, "What literary group met at the Eagle and Child pub, familiarly known as the Bird and Baby?"

My stomach muscles tensed and my thighs trembled. I knew this….

Angel stroked deep inside me. I wasn't just having trouble thinking—I was losing language completely.

The music dum-de-dummed closer to the finish.

My body thrummed closer to orgasm.

"Oh…fuck…yes…The Inklings!"

The red wash of orgasm crashed over me, my screams drowning out the music and even the answer as my body pulsed and shuddered and succumbed.

There really are no winners or losers in this game. Dimly I heard Angel chuckling. "You forgot to say 'Who were'…." She tsk'd. "When you've recovered, I believe it's my turn."

My liquid limbs would resolidify in a few moments and yes, then it would be her turn. I would make my sweet Angel sing to the heavens as many times as I possibly could.

We'd been together a long time, Angel and me. Long enough to have twins in college—Angel had carried them. Long enough to get married when we were finally allowed to, having known that whole time that it was forever for us. It's easy to slip into routines, to stop paying attention, to get dragged down by life and work and family, once the first heated rush of passion has slowed to a glowing pile of embers.

As *Jeopardy* ended and *Wheel of Fortune*'s audience chant began, the flames rose up again to meet the last rays of the summer sun. We wouldn't let them die down again so easily.

a healthy dose

I STAND AT the window with Professor Vondergraft. His office is on the third floor, and we have an excellent view of the gardens, mature and well-manicured.

It is a far cry from the dull and sterile medical offices in which I have been serving my internship. I've been sent to learn more about this place, determine whether their methods are scientific and safe.

It's spring, and not just the roses are blushing.

"Many of the women come here of their own will," he's saying. "Generally the older ones, frustrated by what they've experienced so far. They want to claim their sexuality, learn what joy their bodies can give them. Some are...encouraged to sign up for the program by their husbands. Others—the younger ones—are sent by their mothers." He tugs on his mustache, thoughtful. "Never the fathers," he murmurs. "Always the mothers."

"Hm," I say, a noncommittal answer. My mind whirls at what he's telling me, even as it skips away from the truth of it.

"Pleasure," he continues. "We show them the true meaning of the word. In a variety of ways, with a variety of…aids…we help them reach the pinnacle." He chuckles. "Over and over again."

"Aids," I repeat, not quite a question, but offering him an opening to elaborate.

"We also have at our disposal the latest technologies. Plus, the men and women who work here are trained in various theories of eroticism and use that knowledge to the fullest extent. We've determined what works best for each woman, but most learn the same thing about themselves: that they have a deeply submissive nature and find a delightful level of joy in experiencing erotic pain. Plus, there's nothing like a healthy dose of humiliation to heighten their pleasure, eh?" he asks jovially.

I say nothing, pretending not to understand.

"For example," he says, "you see that girl down there?"

I cannot deny that I do, although I cannot see her features well. She wears a maid's costume, black with a frilled white apron and cap. The skirt is extremely short, revealing shapely legs and even the barest hint of high, rounded bottom.

She's carrying a tea tray with a cut-glass tumbler on it. Whiskey, probably. There's a gentleman sitting at a garden table, enjoying the sun and grounds as he peruses the daily paper. The girl bends to set down the tray, but just before she does, she suddenly stiffens. Her hands jerk, and the drink sloshes out of the glass.

She manages to get the tray safely on the table, but the gentleman is on his feet in an instant. I cannot hear what he says to her, but she puts her hands behind her back and arranges her stance, her face down. The instaneousness of her submissive pose intrigues me.

Professor Vondergraft opens his hand, and I see the remote control device he holds. I can no longer hide behind the lie of not understanding. My prick understands, and responds accordingly.

"With this, I control the level of her pleasure," he says. "I gave her that little jolt so she'd require chastisement, which that gentleman will happily provide. See, now?"

The girl is bent over, her hands gripping the edge of the garden table. The gentleman has flipped up her flounced skirt. She wears no undergarments, and her bottom is pale and, as I suspected, firm and high, with a lovely curve. He reaches into a satchel by his chair and pulls out a glove, which he slips on, and then retrieves something I can't see. I realize quickly that it's some sort of lubricant, as he begins sawing his finger in and out of her bottom. Her back arches, thrusting her curvy rump in the air.

That she enjoys this invasion is curiously fascinating. I knew that men did, but women? It is a revelation.

When the gentleman is obviously satisfied, he gives me another surprise by reaching over the maid to his drink. It takes me a moment, at this distance, to parse what he's doing. He slides one ice cube, then another, into her proffered bottom.

I discover my mouth is hanging open.

The girl dances on her toes at this ignominious invasion and, no doubt, the frigid, shocking sensations the ice causes, but otherwise she remains in position, dutiful and meek.

I find myself eager to see more.

The gentleman removes his glove, reaches back into the satchel, and produces a wooden paddle.

When the implement first crashes down—for the gentleman does not check his hand or otherwise seek to begin gently—the young woman's head jerks up. At the next blow, she shakes her head, slowly, and lets it sink closer to the table again.

As the punishment continues, she raises one foot, then the other, in what looks to be an excruciatingly slow, sensual dance. I wonder if she's even aware of her own movements.

My mouth has gone dry. Oh, that she would deliver to me a tumbler of whiskey….

Throughout the spanking, Professor Vondergraft works the remote control, explaining as he does that he is repeatedly bringing her close to climax, but not giving her a final release.

"This teaches her to associate the pleasure of arousal with the pain of the spanking. She's been an excellent student thus far; I imagine if I hadn't caused her to spill the drink, she might have done it herself, just to earn the spanking." He smiles like a proud parent. "The public display is also a new excitement for her; she finds it horribly embarrassing to know that people could be watching. I'm sure some are watching now, downstairs, on the patio—she would have seen them as she went out. As I understand it, her greatest humiliation—and greatest joy—is knowing someone else controls her orgasm… and that others are witness to her helplessness."

I watch, my hands in my pockets to hide their trembling. I understand that she hates this and craves it in equal measure.

The gentleman below finishes the spanking. As he puts the paddle away, I can see, even from this distance, the bright red flush on her tender, exposed flesh.

I find it intoxicating, and wish I could see it more closely. I wanted to lay my hand against the sweet curve of her cheek and feel the heat radiate into my palm.

Unbidden, the thought rises: I want to be the cause of that heat, that rosy, swollen evidence of pleasurable pain.

Other parts of her will be swollen, too, I realize. Her nipples, her cunt....

"Here." Professor Vondergraft's voice startles me back to the room. He hands me the remote device. "Toy with her all you like. Just be sure to make her come, though—it's imperative to their health that they have frequent orgasms." He chuckles again. "Ah, yes, that's another use of the device, making them come and come again until they beg for mercy—but that's for another time."

My hands are clumsy, and I don't know the controls well enough to have much finesse. But I enjoy watching her writhe, her hands still gripping the table, her hips undulating as if in a slow-motion fuck against the air. I wonder what she's thinking, whether she cares who manipulates the device pressed against her clit, whether her desperation for release outweighs her humiliation of orgasming, helplessly, in front of so many watching eyes.

Finally I take pity on her, and twist the dial to the maximum.

Her reaction is spectacular. Once again, for a moment she freezes. Then her entire body judders before her hips simply go mad with motion. She remains in position as her thrusts become faster, more frantic....

She thrashes, her head flung back, and even from this height I can hear her high-pitched, keening wail. Her movement jostles the table, causes the drink to spill again, and I wonder if she knows she'll be held accountable, that another punishment is in her future. And I wonder if knowing that makes her orgasm stronger.

I'm surprised at my own nature, as I wait before turning off the device for a long minute after she's come, guessing how excruciating that is against her sensitive nub. I see her take a deep, shuddering breath.

Then she straightens, steps away from the table, and sinks to her knees as the gentleman unfastens his trousers and pulls out his stiff prick. Before she takes him in her mouth, however, she looks over her shoulder, directly at the window in which we stand, and smiles her gratitude.

My own prick surges with heat and need as again my mouth drops open.

It's my fiancée, Trudie.

Did her mother send her? Or did she choose to come here, to put herself in these people's hands?

The questions make my prick throb, impossibly hard, in my trousers.

"Well done, my man," Professor Vondergraft says heartily. "You have a knack for this, most certainly. I might just have to hire you away from whatever firm has you captive right now."

Before I can craft a response to his unexpected suggestion, he continues.

"At any rate, you seem to have taken a shine to this girl—would you like me to have her sent to your room later? As part of her training, of course."

"Yes," I hear myself say, "that would be absolutely lovely. Thank you ever so much."

rock-n-roll fantasy

WE ALL YEARN for him, and he flirts will all of us from the stage, making us each feel special, the center of his attention if only for a moment.

When he comes close, I lose myself in tiny details. The slightly crooked eyetooth, and how his teeth would feel scraping and tugging at my nipple. The strong, blunt fingers, and how they would thrust inside me, curving to play my G-spot like a heavenly chord. The faint stubble on his cheeks that would rasp against my inner thighs, and the silk of his hair that curls long at his collar, perfect for me to tangle my fingers in and pull him in closer.

Does he know, as he spins and thrusts, sings and plays, what I'm thinking? I'm sure he knows the gist, but does he suspect how detailed my fantasies are? That a flash of his bare, flat stomach makes me want to lick the sweat from it, then work my way further down? That a single frame from one of his videos spun off an entire spanking storyline in my head?

When he takes my hand, does he know how wet my panties are?

Does he wonder if I put on his music loud, my pulse throbbing in time with the bass and his voice a caress across my naked body, and think of him when I press a vibrator against my needy clit.

Does he imagine what I look like when I come?

Does that make him hard?

Because that's the best fantasy of all.

a sensitive sole

MAYA IS UPSTAIRS getting ready for the party tonight. She'll be shimmying into a pair of tight jeans and a little silk top, probably the seafoam green one bordered with oyster-colored lace.

And then she'll slide her feet into a pair of mules with a kitten heel, and off we'll go.

She doesn't know what's really going to happen, though.

When I met Maya, I didn't really get the whole "shoe" thing. I had a few pairs, sure (Okay, fifteen or so. Maybe twenty, tops.), but other than varying heel heights and a couple of kicky party shoes along with my running shoes, I didn't see the point the need for a separate closet just for things to wear on your feet.

I soon learned that Maya never went barefoot. Hence the need for lots of shoes. (At least she *has* an excuse, right?)

Maya, it turns out, has very sensitive feet. Whereas I'm some kind of hippie throwback who loves to pad around barefoot, the only time Maya is shoeless is when she's in bed. She keeps her slippers right by the side of the bed, so as soon as she gets up, she can slip her feet into them and start her day. She even showers in flip-flops.

The first time I found out just how sensitive her feet were—and how she reacted to sole stimulation, we were on the sofa, watching TV. She was lying with her feet in my lap, wearing just a simple pair of flat, slip-on sandals, the kind with nothing more than a jeweled strap between the toes to hold them on.

She'd had a long day, and I'm a nice girl, so I took off one of the sandals, intending to give her a foot massage.

She looked up, startled. "Oh, no, Katie. I—"

Her words degenerated into a groan when I pressed my thumbs gently into the ball of her right food. I knew many people were ticklish, and I've been told I do a stellar job of massaging feet without causing undue tickling.

It was only after a moment or two of kneading that I realized Maya's groans were not just ones that came from major enjoyment of a great foot massage. I looked over at her.

Her nipples were diamond-hard and drilling their way through her thin cotton T-shirt.

Well, wasn't that interesting? I ran one hand along her leg from shapely calf to smooth thigh, and higher, under the short, flippy skirt she wore.

Her panties were, not to put too heavy a point on it, soaked.

As tempting as it was to just dive in and savor the feast before me, I was curious to see how far this fetish of hers went, just how excited I could get her.

So I tried a little nibbling and licking at her toes. She protested weakly about the potential odor, but I assured her everything was fine. Truth be told, she took care of her feet, and even after wearing shoes, they smelled like perfumed powder. She wore iridescent, shell-pink polish that only enhanced the delicateness of her toes.

When I ran my tongue between those toes, she almost rose off the sofa. I could see her stomach trembling.

I couldn't hold back any longer. I didn't even bother to take off her panties; I just pushed them aside, spread her slick lips with my fingers, and ran my tongue along her folds.

Maya had long since lost the ability to be coherent. She babbled as she wrapped her fingers in my hair and pulled me in tight. Her legs tangled around mine, and I felt her lovely toes digging into my calves as I buried my face between her legs.

Her clit was a hard bud, desperate for attention, and I lapped and licked, urging her higher. I slid two fingers into her hot pussy, and she clenched down hard. When she came, she fluttered and pulsed around me, her clit shivering deliciously against my lips.

Sensitive feet, hm? How could I not take advantage of that? Maya was a luscious thing, lanky and long-limbed, with pale red hair that brushed her shoulder blades, a perky ass, and tasty all over. I was already half in love with her.

By the time we'd moved in together, I'd learned how to exploit her tender tootsies.

One night, after she fell asleep, I moved her slippers, and put a furry sheepskin rug by her side of the bed. When she got up and blearily felt around with her toes, she didn't find what she expected. Her long, low moan was what woke me.

I bent her over the bed, her feet buried in the thick sheepskin, and fucked her with a glass dildo until she was hoarse from crying out.

Last week, I convinced her to let me tie her down. Nothing scary, just a bunch of silk scarves, which I trailed over her body and between her toes before I made sure she was comfortable and knotted them to her hands and the headboard.

Then I got sneaky.

I pulled out a pair of vibrating panties, the kind with the egg in a little pouch that snugs up against your clit, and slid them on her. I turned the dial on the remote to a low setting, to warm her up.

She assumed I'd tie her legs to the bedposts so I'd have access to her sweet pussy. Imagine her surprise when I looped a scarf around both her ankles, binding them loosely together. Then, as a final touch, I wound the ends around her big toes, tying them together so she couldn't pull her feet apart at all.

I crawled up and kissed her, made sure she was okay. There was a little bit of fear in her eyes, but a whole hell of a lot of arousal, too. She whispered for me to keep going. I cuddled her and played with her nipples, and she squirmed; between that and the hum of the vibrator, she was getting close already.

I started with a foot massage, gentle pressure at first, then a bit harder, pulling on each toe, digging my fingers into her arches. I followed that by trailing my fingernails from heel to toe. Her moans increased. I nudged the vibrator to the next level.

Then I pulled out the feathers and went to work on her vulnerable soles. Her entire body went rigid, but she didn't try to escape, didn't try to squirm away, oh no. She was in heaven.

I turned the vibrator on high and watched the fireworks begin.

She almost broke the bed, straining against the silk scarves that bound her as the orgasms wracked her body. Watching her scream and writhe and grind down made me dizzy and oh, so very hot.

When she recovered, she scrabbled in her nightstand drawer until she found our strap-on. She buckled the strap around her waist and ran her hand down the thick, red dildo, then she pushed me down on the bed and went to work on me. I was already drenched from playing with her, from watching her come so hard, that the fake cock slid right into me, deep, just how I like it. I could smell my arousal, mingled with the remnants of hers.

If I knew how to play her, she knew just as well how to play me. I didn't have any specific triggers like she did—I'm happy with plain old fucking, really—but she'd figured out the subtleties.

She urged my legs up on her shoulders so the dildo could go to its maximum depth, banging up against my g-spot and making me scream. She tweaked my nipples, hard, like I liked it, and she pressed her thumb on my clit and made me come, and come again.

And tonight? Well, what she doesn't know is that the party's at a house where they don't allow guests to wear shoes inside. She's going to have to walk around barefoot the entire time, feeling all those different textures on her soles: cold marble, smooth tile around the pool, thick carpet. Maybe a little roughness on the driveway as we get into the car afterwards, because I'm not giving her back her shoes. Once we're in the car, I'll give her the slippers I've had made for her—lined with soft, tickly bunny fur.

Then, when we get home…I've picked up on of those little wheels from the sewing shop—the type with sharp teeth that you press into the paper patterns. I think I'm going to have to tie Maya's ankles down again before I gently roll the prickly wheel along her hypersensitive soles.

I can already imagine how her toes will curl, how her feet will quiver. I can almost hear her squeals turning into screams.

She's never quite been able to come just from foot play alone.

Tonight I plan to change that.

water

WATER. THAT'S WHAT does it for me.

The sluicing heat of a shower. Ocean waves, relentlessly rocking. A pounding, pulsing waterfall. Bodies tangled together in a bubbling Jacuzzi cauldron.

And it's not just water. A steam room, dripping like a tropical jungle. Snow pressed against goose-pimpled skin, hardening my nipples to painful, begging peaks. Honey, dribbled on bare flesh and licked away by an insistent tongue.

Once I was on top, riding hard, on a sultry summer night. I felt each individual bead of sweat trickle down my back, from between my shoulder blades to just above my ass. They triggered a series of deep, volcanic orgasms, one rolling lava flow after another.

So, then, there's this:

A pool, fed by a mountain spring, deep enough in the forest to be secluded, private, untouched. Sunlight dapples the water like fairy sprites; the trees whisper of magic when the breeze strokes their leaves.

The surface is sun-warmed, and I float there, hair spreading around me. The slow current turns me, languid. I can taste the scent of damp earth and pine.

Then, I sense I am being watched.

He poises against a mossy rock, resting half-raised out of the water. Hair sleek like an otter's pelt. His chest and arms are muscled flesh; I cannot tell if his torso ends in legs or a tail.

It doesn't matter.

I tread water, using my legs to keep me afloat, and open my arms, answering, inviting.

He swims into my embrace.

With him, I can breathe beneath the water. We tumble down in a slow, floating dance, coming together in a tangled-tongue kiss, drifting apart so our fingers are the only things that touch.

The water is over me, under me, a lover's touch on every inch of my flesh. And he is like water, fluid and graceful, gliding across my skin. I am wet, outside and in.

His mouth closes over my nipple, and my moan sends bubbles, like tiny messages, to the surface. I watch them break against the rippling barrier above us. He sucks, teeth grazing, and I shudder. I wrap my legs around his waist, struggling to press myself against him, against anything, to relieve the building pressure.

Hands and mouth against both breasts. I arch back, body bowed, buoyed by the water.

He releases me, and though the water is like a lover's touch, I want more. He dives beneath me, swims teasingly between my legs. I twist, somersaulting, but he slips from my grasp. Then he is back, and I sink deeper, taking him into my mouth. He is sleek and slick, cool from the water, and I warm him to an even harder erection.

He slips away again, only to slide along me, against me, until we're facing each other again. His cock teases against my opening, and I spread my legs, near-desperate to feel him inside.

He obliges. When he fills me, I scream a flurry of bubbles, the sound curiously muffled and distorted. I stretch out, as if floating on my back, and he stays vertical, holding on to my hips as he thrusts into me, firm hard strokes.

My hands are free to slip between us. One to encircle him as he slides almost all the way out, the other to stroke my needy clit. I am wet, inside and out, and my fingers slip against the hard bud until the pressure builds greater than I can bear.

I come, dissolving.

peppermint stick

"YOU'RE AWFULLY IMPATIENT tonight," she said. "That's something we'll have to work on."

She doesn't normally restrict my orgasms. It's just something we play with occasionally. My "punishment" for coming too soon will, happily, result in more orgasms anyway. But the point is control, and obedience, and I always try very, very hard to follow her orders.

It's just those damn carolers!

She has me tied up in the living room, just out of sight of the front door. The cuffs are attached to a hook that normally suspends a spider plant. For the season, she's dressed me in white spike heels, a white leather bustier, and angel wings and a halo. A ball gag keeps me from protesting too much. Christmas bells dangle jauntily from my nipple clamps.

Earlier, she amused herself by having me dance to make the bells chime in time to "Jingle Bells," which of course made the clamps all the more effective in teasing my aching nipples.

She lubed up a vibrator and slid it slowly into me, strapped it in, and turned it on low. Not enough to make me come, not yet.

She'd just gotten started with the paddle when the doorbell rang, and I had to wait, aroused and dripping, through "God Rest Ye Merry Gentlemen," "Silent Night," and, ironically, "It Came Upon a Midnight Clear."

When they left, she came back and picked up where she'd resumed. My ass—I could imagine how its redness contrasted with my white outfit—heated nicely in contrast to the cold outside.

The doorbell rang again.

"Here Comes Santa Claus." Lucky bastard.

She removed the clamps, massaging away the flashes of pain, then replaced them, flicking them back and forth so they swayed torturously.

The third time the doorbell rang, my frustrated noises were clear even beneath the gag.

"You're awfully impatient tonight," she says. "That's something we'll have to work on."

She unbuckles the gag, and replaces it with the long end of a peppermint candy cane.

"When you finish sucking every bit of that, you can come," she says. "No biting or chewing allowed. It all has to melt."

To make matters worse, she turns up the vibrator a little bit more before answering the door.

I slurp and suck as fast as I can. I discover almost immediately that I can't go too fast. The peppermint stick nearly slides out of my mouth, and I lunge forward (with the tiny range of motion I had) and catch it just in time.

The bells on the clamps jingle merrily. Swinging back and forth, they twist my tormented nipples.

She glances in from the foyer, expressionless.

God, it's only December twenty-first. She's promised me special torture for each of the Twelve Days of Christmas, and those don't even start for four days.

My world narrows to the delicious bite on my breasts, the buzzing thickness in my cunt, and the hot taste of peppermint in my mouth.

I've always crunched candy canes. I've never been one for patience, which is why this is so hard for me... I keep catching myself before the automatic desire takes hold, torn between giving in to my arousal and holding out until the candy cane is gone.

I just need to come so bad.

I try to distract myself by looking at the tree. The festive multicolored lights blink on and off. Random patterns. But the more I watch, the more they look like they're pulsing.

The throb in my sympathetic nipples begins pulsing in time.

I close my eyes, concentrate on sucking.

Surely I must be close to the end.

Don't check. It'll be longer than you think.

I can't help myself. I check.

Fuck.

She returns then, only to bump up the vibrator another few notches. Oh God, no. I moan around the candy cane, and she pats my cheek. Then she wraps a white, furry mask over my eyes. So I can't see the candy cane. And so I won't know if she's watching me.

We have an open plan house—when she goes into the kitchen or to the front door, she can still see me. If she's in the living room, she'll hear and see if I crunch the candy cane.

The increased vibrations are driving me insane. I'm sure I can feel my juices oozing out, trickling down my leg.

I twist as much as I can, trying to relieve the pressure. Of course, that just adds to the torment. The vibrator fills me, stretches me, and now I'm even more aware of it.

Aware of how the base of it tickles my clit.

Aware of how close I am, how frantic I am.

I feel the hair on the nape of my neck stand up. I can't take this much longer. Is she watching, knowing my limits, enjoying my desperate predicament. My thighs tremble as I try not to come.

Which also makes it worse. Pushes me closer.

Surely I'm almost done with the candy cane?

The tip of the cane touches my cheek. I'm only at the curve. I still have to work my way all around.

But it's already too late. Like one of those spiral lighted trees, the orgasm uncoils inside me. My hips circle, thrust as I spasm uncontrollably around the thick vibrator. The nipping at my tender nipples, the sound of the bells, drive me helplessly on.

Red and white flashes behind my blindfolded eyes.

As I come, my teeth clamp down on the candy cane. The sharp mint crunch mingles with my frantic squeals, and then with the sound of her voice.

"You're in trouble now."

She removes the mask.

Just the sight of the crop, wrapped with red and white ribbon like another peppermint stick, is enough to set me off in convulsions again.

And the Solstice is the longest night of the year…

after the rain

"UM, WOULD YOU mind having dinner with me?"

I looked up, startled, pushing my glasses up my nose. It had been dead quiet this morning, with no new guests were due to arrive, that I hadn't expected anyone to come to the front desk. I was there in case of emergencies.

This didn't sound like an emergency.

The woman asking the question had arrived several days ago, traveling alone from Australia. She was tall and solid, with a ruddy face from lots of outdoor activity and long, wheat-blonde hair.

I confess I developed an immediate crush on her, and not just because of the accent, either. But how could she know that I…?

"I'm sorry," she said with a laugh that filled the high-ceilinged, wood-beamed lobby. She stuck her hand over the counter. "I'm Brianna."

"I know," I said. Lame, oh so lame.

"Oh, of course you do," she said, still with amusement sparkling in her voice. "You checked me in." She always seemed to be happy, really, despite the hideous weather and the fact that there had been no hiking for days and everyone was cooped up in the hotel and going a bit stir crazy. There were only so many board games a bunch of outdoorsy-types could play before things got ugly.

"Anyway," she went on, "I know this seems kind of forward, but you see, the men around here think because I'm alone that I'm desperate for their company, and I'm sick of fending them off. So if you have dinner with me, maybe they'll stop circling like brain-damaged Tasmanian devils."

It took a little wind out of my sails. She wasn't flirting with me; she wasn't asking me on a date. She had no idea I was interested in her.

Then again, the chance to spend some time with her was more than I could pass up.

"Seven o'clock?" I asked.

"I'll make the reservation," she said, and walked away.

Damn, but she could make khaki cargo pants and hiking boots look sexy. The tight white tank top helped, as did the button-down maroon shirt, which was unbuttoned far enough to frame the rounded swell of her breasts. Yum.

I went back to my busy-work of shredding three-year-old marketing material. It was early in the season yet, which meant the lodge didn't have many guests. With the steady, pouring rain drumming on the roof for the last three days, I didn't have to organize any hikes or answer questions and hand out maps.

If it hadn't been for my fantasies about Brianna, I would have been going as stir-crazy as everyone else.

*

We ate in the main dining room. The décor matched the rest of the lodge: rustic rough-hewn logs and beams, evergreen-hued cushions and drapes. The hotel was far from rustic, of course—in its heyday, it had been one of the Great Camps, a summer home for the rich industrialists who came up from the city to experience nature.

Which also explained why there was nothing else for miles around. It wasn't as if the bored hikers could pop into town easily—although some did make the two-hour round trip, only to find that the "town" didn't amount to much more than a grocery store, gas station, and hunting-supply shop (which was closed because it wasn't hunting season. You could get your fishing bait at the grocery store.). It was another hour to the next, larger town, but who'd want to navigate the back roads in this weather?

Brianna peppered me with questions as we waited for our food. How long had I lived in the area? (All my life, except for college in Vermont.) What did I do for fun? (Other than out-door activities—for which, obviously, we shared a passion—I was grateful for satellite dishes and amazon.com.) Which led to favorite TV shows and books, that sort of thing.

I had the fresh trout, breaded crisp on the outside and flaky tender within, feeling vaguely bad for whomever had had to stand out in the deluge to catch it. Brianna ordered the steak, digging into the juicy meat with cheerful gusto.

I took advantage of her eating to get in a question of my own.

"Do you always travel solo?"

She shook her head. "My girlfriend and I booked this holi-day months ago," she said.

Girlfriend meant a friend who was a girl. A best mate, as Brianna would phrase it. Right? I didn't get my hopes up. Then she added,

"But we broke up a couple weeks before we were due to leave, and I couldn't find anyone who could take so much time off from work on such short notice." She shrugged. "So I came by myself."

I barely heard her. I was still stuck on "broke up," which not even Australians said about friends. She really had meant *girlfriend*. Hooray! Maybe I stood a chance.

But despite the bottle of oaky merlot we split, and the brandies we sipped in front of the fire, we didn't get any farther than talking. She touched my knee once when she was telling a particularly impassioned story, but that was it.

Oh well. Despite all the things we found to talk about, I suppose I shouldn't be surprised that she wasn't interested in me. She was gregarious and boisterous; I was a quiet homebody. She was a seasoned world traveler, whereas I hadn't been out of the northeast United States (unless you counted the one trip to Disney World when I was a kid).

It didn't stop me from frigging myself to sleep that night, hearing her sexy accent in my ears and imagining her strong thighs twining with mine as we ground into each other.

*

The next day, miraculously, the sun won its war with the clouds and banished the rain. Many of the trails would be mud pits but at least the guests could get outside and explore, or go down to the lake to use the kayaks.

I wasn't scheduled to work, but they called me in for a few hours in the morning to help get everyone sorted with trail information and whatnot. I didn't see Brianna, and assumed she'd already headed out. I was climbing into my truck to go home—I had a cabin a few miles away—when I heard her lilting accent calling my name.

"They said you had the afternoon off," she said. "I was hoping we could do some hiking together."

I didn't have the heart to ask if it was because the men were bugging her again. I was just happy to have the opportunity to spend more time with her, and to share my little niche of the world with her.

"Hop in," I said. As we bumped down the dirt road littered with water-filled potholes, I explained, "I was going to hike on my own property—I thought you might like to see some scenery that most visitors don't get to see."

I didn't mean it as a double entendre, but she waggled her eyebrows at me. She laughed as she did, though, and I didn't take her seriously. Still, my panties were damp by the time we arrived at my cabin, just from being in her proximity, from listening to her voice and smelling her tea tree oil shampoo.

The wood smelled fresh after all the rains, and everything glittered with an unusual clarity. I pointed out birches and ferns, jays and squirrels (both seen and heard) as we hiked, and talked about how different it looked in the fall, with the brilliant, vibrant colors, and in the winter, when snow blanketed the ground and decorated the bare branches.

In the distance we heard a sound like wind through the leaves, although wind doesn't usually grow louder as you approach. Brianna glanced at me several times, but didn't ask, and I didn't tell—I wanted it to be a surprise.

We rounded a corner and got our first view of the falls.

They weren't particularly high, not by world standards, but they were awfully pretty, and they were mine. Oh, the locals knew about them, and occasionally skinny-dipped in the pool below (but only in the height of summer, when the water was merely bone-chilling, as opposed to freezing-your-ass-off cold).

The look on Brianna's face made it all worth it. She was enraptured, tilting her head up to feel the fine mist caress her skin.

"It's brilliant!" she said. "Simply gorgeous."

I beamed as if she'd been complimenting my offspring, thrilled that I'd been able to share my special place with her.

At which point, she turned to me, took my face in her hands, and kissed me.

Not a friendly thank-you kiss, either. A bona fide making-out kiss. I went from startled to elated as her warm lips moved against mine, as her tongue teased its way into my mouth and met mine. I met her twist for turn, savoring the spearmint on her breath.

When we broke apart, gasping, she gave her sparkling laugh.

"Thank goodness I was right about you!" she said. "I wasn't sure if you were interested."

"I wasn't sure *you* were," I said, and then we were both laughing.

Shortly thereafter, we stopped laughing because we were kissing again.

The water was far too cold to even consider playing in, but a reasonably flat rock where I often relaxed had a soft coating of moss on it, and would do just fine. I don't remember who got who down on it first, but I do know her legs were getting tangled with mine and it was even better than I'd imagined.

Our lovemaking wasn't particularly graceful, what with my shorts getting caught on my hiking boots and moss getting so ground into her bra that she'd never get the green stains out, and the rock poking at least one of us uncomfortably at all times. But it didn't matter. What mattered were her pale, mouthwatering nipples, her jutting hips, her ass just made for fondling, and the thatch of reddish blonde hair at the juncture of her thighs, darker than her hair.

I headed there intending to pack a picnic lunch and spend the day, as they say. She was slippery wet, and tasted exotic, even though I knew logically that she shouldn't taste different just because she was from down under.

This gave "down under" a new meaning. When I giggled, she moaned louder, and I got back to business.

Her cries of pleasure startled a flock of crows, which shot up from the treetops in with a sudden, offended flurry of motion and sound.

*

We said our farewells a few days later, after a blissful spell of outdoor activity and indoor romping (and vice versa). She was scheduled to hit Yellowstone next, followed by the Grand Canyon and Yosemite, before flying home.

I started a new savings account the day after she left, and I'm putting all the money in it I can. Next spring, I'm going to Australia.

Brianna says she's an excellent tour guide.

bathing beauty

IT ALL STARTED because Paul's mother was an Esther Williams fan.

He grew up watching the sleek swimmer, respectful and fascinated by strong, independent, creative women.

And rubber bathing caps.

I didn't actually learn this about him until we found an old poster of Esther in an antiques-and-collectibles shop at the shore. We had a funky and eclectic décor, and I thought the poster was neat, too, so we bought it and had it framed and hung it on our sun porch, which had something of a nautical theme already.

It wasn't until I came home early from shopping with the girls one day and found Paul masturbating to the poster that I suspected that anything was up.

I wasn't upset, or even concerned. We had a healthy sex life, and hey, sometimes a guy (and even a girl) has gotta take matters into his own hands. In fact, the sight of him sitting there, cock red and slick in his fist, made me feel frisky enough to dive in and help out.

I knelt between his legs and took the hot, hard length of him into my mouth.

He'd been at it long enough that his own sweet pre-come mingled with the mostly flavorless lubricant he'd used. I flicked my tongue against the little hole to coax out more of the sweet liquid. He whispered "Oh, yeah," and caressed my hair, not quite pulling me down harder on him, but encouraging me to continue at will.

It wasn't long before I felt his balls tense and heard his breathing catch, and I knew he was on the edge. My pussy tingled in empathetic response (knowing too that he'd return the favor) as I coaxed out his pleasure. I looked up at him as he came, and saw his eyes were wide, and fixated on the poster.

*

I asked him about it later, when we were in bed, and he confessed everything like a naughty schoolboy who always knew—and even half-hoped—that his secret would be discovered.

Esther had consumed his boyhood fantasies, featured heavily in his adolescent longings. His first wet dream had been of her (and we both laughed at the pun in that). Finally, out of erotic desperation, he'd stolen his mother's rubber bathing cap. It was lime green, he said, with big flowers sprouting off of it. Hideous. But compelling.

He knew he couldn't give it back to her afterwards, so he said the dog had chewed it up. He kept it hidden in his mattress for years, brought out only in the dead of night.

Paul was a little hesitant as he told me the story, watching for my reaction, having to be coaxed to tell all the details. We'd been happily experimental when it came to sex, but he'd worried that this was a little farther over the edge than I'd be interested in. I knew, too, that he'd feared tainting the adolescent fantasy. I reassured him, and in the end he said he was glad to be able to tell me.

What he didn't know is that I was already mentally plotting a nice sticky fun birthday surprise for him.

*

Thankfully, I had time to prepare, because it took me a while to find exactly what I needed. I wasn't even sure it existed. But it did: a retro water skiing show, the kind with people stacked in a pyramid, like in the Go-Go's "Vacation" video.

Best part was, they wore bathing caps.

Not rubber ones, alas, but close enough for my purposes and, I hoped, Paul's desires. From afar, it wouldn't really be easy to tell what the elaborate headdresses were made of. It was the show that counted.

Plus there'd be synchronized swimming. And proper bathing caps or no, that had to count for something. It was an Esther Williams fan's dream come true.

When Paul woke on his birthday morning, I greeted him with a kiss, cappuccino, a bagel with cream cheese and lox, and a card that told him he was going to have a special day.

Lunch was a lovely meal at a prime seafood restaurant at the shore, and then we were off to the show.

Paul had a mix of mild confusion and burgeoning lust on his face when he realized what we were about to see. I snuggled up against him and breathed into his ear, "This is your special day, honey. Enjoy."

He enjoyed, all right. More than once I saw him adjust himself, and for a while even lay his program over his lap to ensure innocent bystanders weren't treated to an eyeful. I was tempted to bring him off right there at the show, but the bleachers weren't exactly set up for any modicum of privacy, and it would kind of spoil the occasion to get arrested for public indecency.

I had other, better plans.

In the parking lot, he backed me up against the car and kissed me, his tongue darting into my mouth in a way that makes me think only of how that would feel on my clit (and I always knew that pleasure would be forthcoming). He pressed his hips against mine, and I felt the outline of his hard cock against my mound.

"Thank you, sweetheart," he said when we broke for air. "That *was* special."

"Oh, we're not through yet," I said, unable to keep the teasing glee from my voice. "This was just…foreplay."

I swear I felt his cock twitch against me. We decided I should be the one to drive home, just to be safe.

*

It wasn't long before I had Paul naked and stretched out on our bed, his cock at half mast, pulsing towards full erection as he imagined what erotic surprises I might have in store for him.

He'd been a competitive swimmer in high school and college, and had the body for it: long and lean with sleek, seal-like muscles; broad shoulders and narrow hips; and mostly hairless, so he hadn't had to shave his chest and legs like some of his teammates. Indeed, I'd always been hot for the way he looked in a Speedo, the shiny Lycra outlining the taut dimples in his hips and the heavy soft package of his penis and balls cupped in the front.

I didn't think I had a rubber fetish myself, but I found myself wondering how his groin would look encased in rubber. Deep royal blue, to bring out his eyes.

As if I'd be looking at his eyes.

We'd played with cock rings before—simple leather adjustable ones—so I figured a slightly stretchy rubber one wouldn't be too much of a step up. I rolled it down Paul's cock, gently tucked it behind his balls. Now he was fully hard, his cock like velvet-covered steel in my hands.

He reached for me, nuzzling my breasts before grazing his teeth across my nipples, just the way I like it. I'd been wet all day, really, just imagining how this would go, and now a fresh wave of desire shimmered through me, from nipples to clit. I wanted more.

That's when I pulled out the bathing cap.

Yep, I'd found one of those old rubber ones, It wasn't lime green, unfortunately, but white, with a couple of red and blue flowers on one side that gave it the look of a cloche hat from the 1920s.

Paul sucked in his breath when he saw it. With a deliberately lewd grin, I sprawled back on the bed and stretched it across my pussy. "Dive in," I suggested.

He didn't need further encouragement. He rarely did, but this time he was like a man possessed, breathing in the rubbery smell as he found my clit.

It wasn't long before I needed more, though. The material was just too thick for me to get full sensation—and I needed it right now. I pulled the cap away, and he paused, just for a moment, to turn it over and run his tongue along the side that had been against me, tasting my juices coating the rubber. His eyes were closed, his face worshipful. Then he turned back to me, and he gave me the same worshipful attention.

I held the cap across his neck and used it to pull him closer as my thighs started to tremble. My orgasm wasn't long in coming, but I could feel every second, every degree of it as the erotic sensations pooled in my groin. My legs, my stomach tightened, and then the flick of Paul's tongue against me finally pushed me over the edge.

It took me a moment to recover, but when I did, it was time to focus on him.

To my amazement—and, I'll confess, delight—I almost sent Paul over the edge when I rubbed the bathing cap across his nipples. I knew he was sensitive there, but the feel of the rubber heightened things exponentially. I expect the cock ring was the only thing that kept him from coming from the nipple play alone.

Well. He was close, and I wanted to bring him off so much my clit was tingling again in anticipation. I trailed the cap across his balls, watching as they jumped. Listened to his breath hissing between his teeth.

I slipped my hand into the cap and drizzled rubber-friendly lube across it, and then, using it almost like a mitten, wrapped it and my fingers around his steely cock.

He cried out my name, his hips rising off the bed. Just a few tight strokes, and he was pulsing and twitching, his come mingling with the lube, the musky scent mingling with the rubber smell, and I think I had a sympathetic mini-climax just from watching him and hearing him.

You'd think that would be enough. But we played long into the night. I don't know…I didn't think rubber was my thing. Still, there's this bra-and-panties set I've found online, in a jaunty red, that I've got my eye on…

taming his wild cat

SHE LIKED TO scratch, which is why he called her his little wild cat.

It was harder to scratch him when he encased her hands in mittens that looked like feline paws.

She liked to hiss, which is also why he called her his little wild cat.

It was harder to hiss with a gag in her mouth, one with whiskers sprouting from the strap. The gag went so well with the headband bearing spotted felt cat's ears.

If she couldn't scratch or hiss, then she couldn't complain when he buckled a collar around her neck.

"Of course," he said, "I also have to bell my cat." He dangled the shiny silver clamps in front of her, and she batted at them, making the little bells chime. He laughed, then tugged on her rosy nipples until they pouted, and tightened the clamps around them.

She growled, deep in her throat, when he lubed her ass and slipped in a butt plug—one with a curling cat tail attached. He tickled her inner thighs with the end of the tail, just to watch her writhe.

He flipped the switch. The plug began to vibrate.

That's when his little wild cat arched her back and began to purr.

come as you are

"WE'RE GOING TO try something new," I said, keeping my tone conversational as if I were discussing a recipe I'd seen in a magazine, as if I weren't standing behind Connor and fastening cuffs around his wrists.

His fingers flexed, as if he wanted to fist his hands, but he knew better than to do that. His knuckles brushed the curve of his high, tight ass, and I paused for a moment to enjoy the sight of the rich green leather against his pale skin and, below, the fading red stripes from the crop not long ago.

I liked watching his ass flex when I cropped him.

"Something new," I repeated, moving to stand before him. His head was bowed, as appropriate. I was tempted to tuck my forefinger under his chin, nudge his gaze up so I could watch his expression. But I suspected I'd see his reaction in another way. "No fucking," I said. "No hands. Just your mouth on me, making me come."

His reaction was so swift it made me smile. His cock, half-hard already because of the cuffs, surged as if it had a mind of its own.

Connor loved to go down on me. Love to worship my clit, my slick lips, loved to taste me and lick me and suck and nibble until my thighs clenched and I pulsed and sometimes I squirted. He loved my scent, the feel of me on his mouth, and it was something I frequently exploited, to both our delight.

But this…this would be different. Because usually afterwards, we fucked—more often than not, with me on top, enjoying a few more orgasms before I allowed Connor his release. (Well, no matter position I chose, the latter was true.)

What I wasn't going to tell him—not just yet—was that I wanted to see if he could come just from the pleasure of going down on me.

Because I wanted to see how quickly he'd figure that out on his own.

Now, his hands securely bound, I settled myself back on the settee against a mound of pillows, spread my legs, and beckoned him to me. I felt like a queen, an object of worship—and, truly, that's how Connor approached me. We'd talked about it, early in our relationship, about how he wanted a woman he could devote himself to fully and completely, someone to love and cherish and, yes, worship. To him, I was to be adored, venerated, and I reveled in that, even as I respected that my dominion over him, as it were, came with responsibility.

That's what love is all about, isn't it?

So he approached me on his knees, subservient and obsequious, and I tilted my hips towards his eager mouth.

Slow, at first. I'd had to teach him that. Even if a woman was already aroused, she didn't want to be pounced upon and wildly devoured—she wanted to be savored, wanted the pleasure to build.

Oh, certainly sometimes I wanted to come faster than others, and I could instruct Connor to ramp things up quickly. The operating phrase being "ramp things up."

Now, he first inhaled the scent of my arousal, his eyes fluttering closed as he savored it. Then he leaned farther forward to place a gentle kiss before his tongue swirled through my lips and around my clit with a gentle reverence.

I was torn, wanting to let me head drop back and just revel in the sensations, but also wanting to watch. I loved seeing his face buried in my crotch.

"*Very* good, Connor," I murmured as he licked every inch of me with long, slow strokes. "Such a talented tongue." I could feel the blood pooling in my groin, the delicious heaviness as my arousal built.

"I said something new, didn't I?" I went on, my toes crimping the sheet on the settee as I tensed. "I said no fucking, no hands. But we've done that before."

Connor didn't respond. He knew what his task was, knew the punishment for slacking.

"I didn't mean just what you're doing to me—oh *God*, just there." I was getting close. I hadn't timed this as well as I would have liked. Connor was just so talented! "I mean I won't be fucking you, either. Or using my hand on you. Or you using your hand on yourself."

I thought I heard a faint, querulous noise.

"It's going to go like this," I said. "When I come, you may come. In fact, when I come, you are *required* to come."

His tongue stuttered just then, a brief startled pause as the weight of my words sank into his sub-spaced brain.

I rested a hand on his head, reminding him of his duty.

My clit throbbed gently; I was on the edge. A part of me wanted to something inside of me—Connor's fingers, a dildo—but I'd said no hands, and that was the fun of it for both of us. Connor was well able to make me come, hard, just from using his mouth.

"I'm getting close, Connor. Are you? I know you're hard—you always get deliciously hard when you lick me, like a good boy. Are your balls tight? Are you getting close, too? I'll be very disappointed in you if you don't come when I tell you to, you know. We'll have to figure out a suitable punishment." My words were coming in gasps now. "Orgasm restriction, maybe, or maybe I'll tie you up and make you come over and over again until you can't stand it."

The mental images of Connor begging, his cock red and swollen—in either scenario—were enough to tip me over that wonderful edge. My groin flooded with warmth as my clit pulsed. My hips involuntarily raised off the bed and I ground myself into Connor's face.

Lost in the throes of my own orgasm, for a few moments I wasn't precisely aware of Connor. When I was able to open my eyes and focus, he drew back and sat up, his chest heaving.

The sheet I'd draped over the settee glistened with his ejaculate.

"Oh, Connor, well done." I stroked his chiseled face with my fingertips. "You've passed this first test so well…"

devouring heart

THE MUSIC THROBBED, a heavy beat that spoke of dark things. Dark things that, like the music, got under your breastbone and lodged there, pressing rhythmically against your heart. Most of the lights in the club were red, making everyone look as though they had been doused with fresh blood.

It was like being inside a pulsating heart. I moved through it, aorta and ventricle and life-affirming beats, looking for Sorcha.

Sorcha first walked into the club two years ago. I remember the night, of course. Everyone turned to stare, because she was gorgeous.

Straight, blue-streaked black hair down to her ass. Said ass was delectable, covered in a leather miniskirt over ripped fishnets. She wore a white baby-doll top that depicted a mouth biting into a broken heart. The shirt was skintight and a size too small, revealing a slice of pouty tummy and outlining a pair of pierced nipples.

I wanted nothing more than to rub my own breasts against those cold rings, to wrap my hands around her tight ass and grind my crotch against hers until we were both screaming incoherently.

But first, I wanted to ask her to dance.

I didn't believe in love at first sight. I'm still not sure I do, not even now. It took me a couple of months to fall in love with her, or so I tell myself. That first night, however, when she walked in, and everybody stared, and everybody wanted her…it didn't matter.

She walked straight up to me.

Dancing was just exquisite, excruciating foreplay for us. Two or three songs later, her pierced tongue was licking my earlobe in time to the driving beat of the music, making me imagine what that would feel like against my clit, which pulsed in the same rhythm. Her hands proved to me that my belly ring made that area a huge erogenous zone for me.

I soared and swam in a sea of scarlet desire.

I took her home that night, and fulfilled those fantasies I was having and then some. Playing with her nipple piercings was enough to make her come, and we discovered her hands were small enough to fit inside of me. When she uncurled her fist in my slippery cunt, my vision bloomed roses, red and black.

I'd had my share of one-night stands, and I told myself I didn't expect her to be much more than that. I'd be happy if she stuck around, but I didn't dare hope for it. At the end of the night, she told me she loved me. When I asked her how that was possible, she said, "I didn't know I was looking for anyone, but when I walked in and I saw you, I just *knew*."

Two years later, it was my turn to walk in looking for her. Because five days ago, she'd disappeared.

I didn't see her anywhere, but it was hard to see through the crush of dancing bodies. I mounted the industrial metal steps up to the bar, where I'd have a better view.

Ambrose, looking dashing as usual in a tuxedo top made out of strips of black and white leather with a bowtie of spikes, handed me a double shot of vodka before I asked. I drank it in one gulp, without a shudder. I couldn't taste anything these days.

"I'm sorry, Case, but you missed her," he said. "She left maybe half an hour ago."

I nodded my thanks to him, paid double what I owed, and left. Outside, I threw the shot glass against the wall, but the sound of shattering glass didn't help. Then I went to Sorcha's house.

She hadn't bothered to lock the front door, not that I couldn't've picked the lock if necessary. I'd done it before, these past five days, to find the place empty. I'd even waited inside all one night, creeping out just before dawn.

If my actions screamed "stalker!" or "crazed ex-lover!" I didn't fucking care, okay? Maybe even crazy stalkers think they have their reasons, think it's all is for the best.

They were in the bedroom, and from the moans of ecstasy, I assumed they were having sex. No reason not to, I supposed. I flipped on the light—Sorcha favored blue bulbs, and it was like peering through a bottle of Curacao, or swimming in a Caribbean sea (not that I'd ever see that). Sorcha was wearing the sapphire satin corset I'd bought her. My gut wrenched, ached more than I expected it to.

Her partner's head shot up, but Sorcha was slower to move, languidly disengaging her teeth from the other woman's wrist.

"Case," she said. She sounded drunk. That's the sensation vampires feel when they're feeding. I'd guessed what had happened to her when she disappeared, and Ambrose had confirmed my suspicions three days ago. If you hang out long enough at the club, you'll get approached with an offer. Not everybody takes it, and I was surprised—stunned—that Sorcha had.

I grabbed the other woman—whose mouth was blood-wet, so I knew she'd already fed—and threw her at the bedroom door. The jamb splintered when she slammed against it.

"Get the fuck out," I snarled. She pulled herself upright and snarled incoherently back, but she left. I heard the front door bang shut.

"Case," Sorcha said again.

"Sorcha, you idiot," I said, kneeling on the bed next to her. "Why didn't you tell me?"

"I was afraid, Case," she said, and I heard the desperation in her voice. "I didn't want—I don't want—"

"Never mind," I said, still with a snarl in my voice. "Just shut up and fuck me."

Our coupling was as violent and incredible as our first. I yanked her sweet breasts out from the corset before she knew what hit her, and I straddled her thigh and used the nipple rings like reins. I rode her, but in truth I wasn't after my own gratification—not yet, at least.

Did I want to punish her for running away from me? Maybe, a little. Punishment for Sorcha was pleasure, so it wasn't as if I was teaching her a lesson.

I couldn't deny her. My knee wedged between her legs but it almost wasn't needed, because she could come just from the way I twisted and tugged the piercings. Her nipples flushed near-purple, and she bucked beneath me, writhing in pain that transmuted into pleasure and back again.

"It's okay," I whispered, my lips pressed against the pulse in her neck.

After that first round of orgasms she had recovered from the feeding and was stronger, so I let her take control. ("It's okay," she'd whispered back, and I'd believed her.) She buckled leather cuffs—blue, like her corset—around my wrists. The cheap gold spray paint had worn away from the wooden headboard wood where the cuffs had been chained time and time again.

She strapped on our favorite black dildo and thrust it towards my mouth. Black dildo, blue satin, blurring into a bruise as I sucked. She knew what I wanted, what I would have begged for if she hadn't been gagging me with the silicone cock, and that was to have it inside me. To have her leaning over me, sweaty and flushed, while she plunged it into me.

But even when she did, she teased and toyed—and restrained, I could do nothing but force my hips harder toward hers, struggling for satisfaction. It wasn't our usual game, but I was so happy to have found her again that even the frustration was mixed with a contradictory sense of relief.

Still, when she pulls the dildo out of me, I swear at her. Nasty terms of endearment. She smiled, just a little, as she promises me what I'm begging for.

She slid a smaller vibrating cock into my ass and slid her face down my body, I assumed to lick my aching clit. Instead she tongued my belly piercing, and I arched my back as best I could, and that's when she pressed another vibrator to my clit. Then all I knew was that I shattered and screamed and ultimately came very, very close to passing out. When I thought I couldn't bear to come anymore, I begged her to stop, insisting I would die even though we both knew that couldn't happen.

She undid one of the cuffs so I could tuck it around her before she fell asleep on my chest. Exhausted, sated, finally back in her arms, I followed her into oblivion.

Which shows just how irrationally desperate I am for a happy ending. As always, I should have known better.

*

I woke to the sandpaper rasp of teeth scraping my neck. I sighed my contentment; so this is what she wanted, after all.

But she'd barely broken the skin before she pulled away, sobbing.

"Sorcha?" I reached out my free hand.

"I'm sorry, Case, but I can't do it. I can't bring you down into this. I know it sounds like the perfect life: never aging, never dying, feasting in the dark." She gave a bark of humorless laughter. "The perfect goth fantasy. But it's not. The killing makes me sick. The drinking is…abhorrent to me. It's disgusting. I can't make you do that, too. I love you, and I want you with me always, but I can't let you suffer with me."

She ran out of the bedroom. A moment later, I saw the bright crack of light between the heavy curtains, and realized it was full morning.

"Sorcha, no!"

I wrenched at the cuff, now a prison, until I heard the headboard crack and splinter. I was halfway down the stairs when Sorcha opened the door. I screamed her name again, and she turned.

"I love you," she said, and stepped backwards into the sunlight and died.

*

I spent the rest of the day in her house, trapped. I lost count of how many times I walked up to that open door and stood there, looking out.

I'd known what had happened to her in those five missing days, and I'd allowed the same thing to happen to me, so we could be together always.

She never gave me the chance to tell her.

But I can't bring myself to step outside. Sorcha, in the end, was far braver than I can ever be.

from bitter to sweet

Taste: Bitter

I saw you with your new girlfriend today. The one you so unceremoniously dumped me for.

I found your favorite vibrator the other day while I was cleaning, and being the honorable person that I am, I wrapped it up to return to you. I even included a bar of your favorite Green & Black's extra dark chocolate.

Is it my fault I forgot and let the package sit on the dash of my car on a hot summer's day?

Filling: Nuts

We reach for the last bag of peanut M&Ms at the same time. My first thought is disappointment, but then I look up and see her smile as she suggests we split the bag. We sit on the pier watching the sunset, and I'm less interested in the candy and more interested in the way she slowly sucks each smooth piece into her mouth, the way her legs stretch out before her, long and lean. Her toenails are painted M&M blue.

I pick out all of the green M&Ms and set them aside. She raises an eyebrow; she knows what they mean. When we've finished eating and the sun has set, I offer them to her.

She sets one on my collarbone and nibbles it off. I feel the sensation of her gentle teeth all the way down between my legs. She suggests we share the rest of them at her place, in private.

Texture: Creamy

Her skin is dusky like toffee, smooth like caramel.

On our fourth date, she set up a fondue pot full of semi-sweet Hershey's morsels, hot and liquid. She dipped strawberries in and fed them to me, holding one end between her full lips and kissing me through the confection. Eventually we abandoned the fruit. She said my nipples were like plump raspberries, and bathed them in melted chocolate before sucking on them.

Later, she told me about Ben & Jerry's Super Fudge Chunk, and what she would do to me with it.

Topping: Marshmallows

I said I hated camping, but she convinced me to go for just one night. Over the crackling campfire, she made real hot chocolate—not powdered, not from a mix. Mayan Hot Chocolate, she said, slicing the chilies and splitting the vanilla beans.

After we drank it, she dragged me into the tent. The burgundy nylon rustled as we evoked the pagan gods and sacrificed ourselves on the altar of our lust.

Taste: Sweet

She slips the chocolate pastille—some astonishingly expensive kind from Switzerland—into my mouth. The dark, sweet taste explodes on my tongue.

"No biting," she instructs. "You have to let it melt. And you can't make any sound until it's all gone."

My tongue screams, but I don't, even as she moves her way down my body. I writhe and sweat, but remain mute like she asks. My world turns dark red, like the inside of a chocolate-covered cherry.

Green & Black's no longer seems exotic. I've almost forgotten your name.

guess who's coming at dinner

"SUPPER'S GOING TO BE a little different tonight," I told Archie.

As if he hadn't figured that out. I mean, he was already tied face up on the coffee table, legs pulled wide, a pillow under his head and another under his ass to give me full access. He was naked, of course.

And I'd spread a plastic checkered tablecloth down before I'd bound him there.

"I've been concerned lately about how you haven't had time for a proper meal," I said. "I know the Hwang account had you busy, but if you don't slow down and enjoy your food…"

"Yes, ma'am," he said. "I'm sorry, ma'am."

"We'll fix that tonight," I said. "You'll take your time and eat a well-rounded meal with me."

"Yes, ma'am."

"First course: fruit salad."

I sampled a slice of kiwi drizzled with honey, savoring the balance of tart and sweet, before feeding him some. He eagerly sucked the sticky remains off my fingers. The feel of his talented tongue on my flesh made me shiver a little.

I was already wet. I'd had the food catered, but just planning the menu and ordering it had started me on the path of arousal, thinking about what I was going to do with it, planning Archie's exquisite torture. Not to mention the act of tying him down. That always gets my nipples hard, my skin flushed and sensitive.

I selected a delectable ripe strawberry, held it delicately by the tiny leaves, and, while Archie watched hungrily, I slid it along my pussy lips, coating it in my juices.

He licked it off before biting into the fruit. "More, please, ma'am," he whispered, and I was only too happy to oblige him. The seeds rasped against my clit as I repeated the action. I almost didn't want to stop.

Farther down, I saw his cock twitching to life.

I spooned some spicy gazpacho soup into his mouth, helped him lift his head so he could sip some oaky white wine. After we both enjoyed some baked potato, I made him suck sour cream off my nipples.

We both enjoyed that even more. I could tell not just from Archie's fervent *thank yous*, but from the way his cock had grown during the first courses of the meal.

"I'm glad you're enjoying this, Archie." I scraped my fingernails lightly along his balls, which jumped under my touch. "Remember, though, that I'm trying to teach you to make time for good, proper meals. I want you to understand the value of slowing down. So just understand..." and here I ran one nail up the sensitive underside of his cock "...you won't get to come until you've finished your supper."

I'm pretty sure I heard a faint whimper, but he didn't say anything. He licked his lips, and from his prone position he tried to look around to see where the rest of the food was, to gauge how long he had to wait.

Silly boy. It had nothing to do with how much food there was. It had to do with when I was good and ready to let him come.

The next dish was probably a cliché, but if it was, it was for a good reason. One can have so much fun with asparagus dripping with hollandaise sauce!

Between eating our share of it, I drizzled the sauce on his chest and licked it off, paying special attention to his nipples, grazing them with my teeth. Now he really *was* whimpering as my mouth closed over those receptive nubs. He could take only so much stimulation there, and I brought him right to the edge of his comfort zone, toying with him long enough to make him wonder how far I'd really go.

Not too far. Not yet. I still had so much planned.

The meal had barely started. We were only just getting to the main course: lobster dipped in butter.

We made quite a mess with that, of course. He cleaned me off as best he could, and I him, teasing and toying with him. The sweet taste of the lobster was almost as good what I was doing with the dish.

It seemed out of synch with the meal's proceedings when I produced a carrot, complete with leafy top. Archie's eyes questioned, but I just smiled and proceeded to sheathe it in a condom and coat it in the drawn butter.

But not before I picked a juicy red apple and stuck it in his mouth.

Archie has a love/hate relationship with anal play. On one level, he resists it; on the other, he craves it. He despises how helpless he became, how affected he is by something long and hard steadily sliding deeper into him. He'll pretend it wasn't there, which was handy—it was almost like bondage without the restraints because he'd try not to move.

But, of course, I would do something that would cause his hips to jerk or grind, and he'd be reminded all over again of the thick object pressing against his prostate, filling him up.

It was utterly delicious, and I took advantage of it whenever I could.

"I can't begin to tell you how delightful the view is," I said. "The green leaves are all bushed out." He groaned around the apple. "I'll bet they're tickling your balls and just driving you crazy."

He didn't respond, but I didn't expect him to. I grabbed my phone and took a shot straight down between his legs, capturing his spread legs, erect cock, and the greenery poking out of him. When I showed him the image, his face flushed the same color as the fruit in his mouth.

His cock was the same hue, belying his facial reaction.

"Would you look at that?" I wrapped my fist around the base of his stiff, reddened member and squeezed upward. Clear liquid drooled out. He pumped his hips, trying to encourage me to do it again, to speed up my tight caress. I knew only a stroke or two more would make him explode, he was so close.

I left my hand clamped on him, unmoving, and removed the apple from his mouth. Selecting another asparagus stalk, I dipped the rough tip into his precome and twirled the spear to coat it.

"Ah God," he groaned. "Please."

"Not yet," I said sternly. "You may be done eating, but I'm not finished with my meal." I made a point of sliding the asparagus between my pouting lips. Slowly. Oh, I know it's almost tacky, but it works all the same. Archie's chest heaved as all he could do was helplessly fantasize that his cock was sliding between my lips instead.

In truth, I wasn't hungry anymore, but I wanted to draw this out as long as possible. Relish the power of being in control, of choosing when to give him his release.

"Since you've finished your main course, how about dessert?" I asked.

I could see him trying to figure out the right answer. I'd told him he'd have no orgasm until he finished eating—but would he annoy me by refusing food I offered him?

"Maybe we could wait," he said, his voice cracking a little from the strain. "Have it later?"

"That's fine with me. We have all night." To emphasize my words, I toyed with the leafy end of the carrot, which jiggled the vegetable inside him. I saw his butt cheeks clench, felt his tortured cock throb in my motionless grip. Oh, he was so very, very close. I wondered idly whether, if I simply told him to, he would come without my even moving.

"No! No, ma'am," he amended quickly. His breath was coming in short pants as he struggled to control himself. "That's not what I meant. I meant dessert…afterwards."

"Impatience will not be rewarded," I said. "If you're honestly full, that's another matter, and I'll trust that you're telling me the truth. In that case, since you've rejected dessert, I suppose you'll have to clean my plate for me," I said, standing up. When I let go of his cock, it bobbed, the blood pulsing in it. "That being a euphemism for cleaning *me*," I clarified as I straddled the table.

"Of course," I added cheerfully before I lowered myself onto his face, "you might consider this to be the same as your dessert."

His muffled moan of pleasure rose from between my legs.

"When you finish—and by 'finish' I mean when you make me come—then you'll be allowed to, too." To emphasize my words, I reached back and tickled the purple head of his cock with another asparagus tip.

For a moment his mouth didn't move. I was pretty sure it was because he was struggling against the tremendous urge to shoot his load right there.

Then he began to lick, his tongue slithering across my lips before homing in on my quivering clit. He was good under any circumstances, but at times like this, when his own pleasure was at stake, he was nothing short of masterful. It wasn't long before I felt my orgasm rise, streaking down my thighs, tightening my stomach, before I was bucking and grinding against his talented mouth.

He'd done his job well, and he deserved reward, which I gave him with my hand slick with melted butter, and very soon slick with his come.

*

Later, as we cuddled, naked and spent, on the sofa, he asked, "What *was* planned for dessert, anyway?"

"Chocolate mousse," I said. I smiled. "But don't worry—we have all weekend."

redemption

HE CAME TO her even in her cell, at her most desperate hour.

She drew back, startled. "I didn't dare hope to see you. They all betrayed me. I thought even He had forsaken me."

"His ways are mysterious, even to me," Michael said. He reached out to her, his great wings folding around her, ever a comfort. "But I would never leave you, Jehanne."

"I am afraid," she said, and the archangel held her while she wept. Hard to believe that the bravest woman in the world, the savior of the French, could be reduced to such despair.

He had been with her since the beginning, along with the saints Caterine and Marguerite, when she was only a child. He had been her confidante, her advisor, her most trusted companion. It was Michael who relayed the messages that God had for her, Michael who translated them for human comprehension.

Now, huddled in a cold, damp cell in Rouen, having been turned over to the hated English by the Burgundians, threatened with rape, charged with heresy, and sentenced to burn, she asked,

"Is it His will that I am to die?"

Michael's arms and wings tightened around her. His silence was her answer.

*

The archangel and the saints came to Jehanne d'Arc when she was twelve, telling her to be pious, go to Church, and, eventually, to help the Dauphin oust the invading Angleterre from French soil. By the time she was seventeen, she was leading an army, with Michael, the former commander of Heaven's armies against Satan Himself, her chief counselor and advisor.

And companion of the flesh.

Jehanne never denied the nickname of *La Pucelle*, for in truth she had never bedded a man, and truly was a Maid. But that did not mean that she had never experienced pleasure; it did not mean that God, through Michael, had not shown her reward for her faith and her actions that pleased Him.

Since coming to the Dauphin, she had worn men's clothing, not as a disguise, but as protection against men. The laces and points that tied together the woolen hosen and cote made it harder for someone to violate her. The benefits of making it easier to ride a horse and gaining a certain amount of respect from the troops were secondary, although no less appreciated.

The English called this heresy, the wearing of men's clothes by a woman. Yet they still forced her to wear them, for when she wore women's clothes in this military prison she fought off the guards again and again. She would have gladly donned a kirtle and cotehardie if they hadn't denied her a proper detainment in a Church-run prison with nuns as her guards.

She was damned either way, in the eyes of the English, but her virginity was still intact.

*

The first time Michael had held her, she hadn't been frightened. She felt only peace in his presence. An archangel was the hand of God, and even though Michael could be terrible in war, he was beautiful in peace. When he kissed her that first time she had trembled, not from fear but from a longing, a desire, that welled up from deep inside her, startling her with its intensity.

Before then, she'd known only such a longing for God Himself, in her heart. This new longing sent heat licking across her flesh, hardened the tips of her small breasts beneath her linen shirt, and caused her very core to liquefy. Tentatively and then with more confidence she returned his kiss, welcoming his tongue into her mouth and tasting his sweet breath.

Michael could remove her clothing with just a look—no need for unlacing—and could replace them just as quickly. Sometimes Jehanne wasn't sure if he were actually removing them or whether he was somehow slipping between them, sliding closer to her. Sometimes she didn't truly know whether he touched her physical body or her soul, for how could her physical body be the source of such pleasure?

He caressed her not only with his hands but also with his wings. The feathers were softer than goose down yet as manipulative as his fingers. When one wingtip brushed against the bud beneath her legs, she cried out the name of God and found greater salvation than she had ever known.

*

Jehanne knew without having to ask that Michael would be with her until the end. Tonight, the night before her execution, she moved in his arms, leaving a trail of moist red bites across his chest. She knew he could heal them instantly, but it pleased them both if he let them stay, a physical reminder of their passion.

Her hated clothes were gone. Feathers caressed her back like the silken sheets she'd enjoyed at the royal palace as his hands moved to her breasts. Her nipples tightened beneath his fingers, and she moaned her excitement. He suckled them as his wings gently slapped her bottom, a whip of downy steel.

"Yes, yes, yes," she moaned in time with each spank, the pain mingling with the pleasure. Hands replaced wings and feathers slid all over her, igniting every inch of her skin until she was a single mass of desire. She was drifting in his arms and yet desperate for one final touch, the stroking that would bring her release.

He lifted her until she was at the height of his face and teased her nether lips apart with his tongue. She writhed in his embrace as he drank her juices, something he so enjoyed. When he finally slid across her aching clitoris, she tensed for an instant and then exploded, with only the archangel's embrace to keep her from flying completely apart.

*

They thought Jehanne burned from the flames, screaming from the pain. But Michael took her beyond all of that. His touch burned her with ecstasy and her shrieks were of delight. He was everywhere: at her breasts, her bottom, the back of her neck, between her legs, teasingly drawing out the sensations, not yet letting her orgasm.

In the final moment, he entered her for the first time. Jehanne shuddered as she was finally one with him, and with God. And on the wings of rapture, they ascended to Heaven.

wasn't it good?

ONE PROBLEM WITH community musical theatre is that the songs say more than you can ever say in life. Characters stand on either side of the stage, oblivious to each other, and pour their hearts out without hearing the other also singing about love or hatred.

In *Chess*, for example, the wife and the girlfriend of Anatoly sing about how neither of them are right for him—that what he wants and needs is the other one.

In the song "Wasn't It Good?", they sing the title question. Good, and fine? They ask each ask whether it's madness that he won't be mine.

The song is the only time the two women appear on stage together, even if they don't acknowledge each other's presence.

That was a damn good thing. Because the other problem with community musical theatre is that you end up being in shows with the same people.

And it was more than a little awkward to be sharing the stage with the wife of the man who used to be yours.

I glanced stage right, but Lori wouldn't meet my gaze.

I could only guess what she was thinking.

Ironically, she had the lead role, that of Anatoly's girl-friend. The wife—my part—didn't even show up until Act II.

One scene together. One song. Her sweet soprano to my strong alto. Our voices weaving, dipping, soaring, intertwining around a single theme of forbidden love, too short and too soon taken away.

No, I *did* know what she was thinking.

Seven years ago, now. During a production of "The Pirates of Penzance." Women in frilled bonnets and flouncy dresses, pretending to be innocent. But what woman doesn't have a weakness for men in pirate outfits, tight pants and open shirts baring an expanse of firm chest?

We were younger then, and daring to the point of foolish. Lust was in the air, not just for us. We probably weren't the only ones who snuck off to the orchestra practice room, "borrowed" key clutched in hand, breathless with danger and desire.

A heady combination.

The darkened room. Barely any space between chairs and music stands and instrument cases. We pressed up against the baby grand piano, gleaming black as night. The cover slapped down over the keys, and we held our breaths until the strings' vibrations faded, and no one knocked on the door.

Wasn't it good?

Fingers fumbling with unfamiliar costumes, frantically groping over the fabric when the fastenings proved too difficult. Nipples so hard, so jutting that they could be tweaked and twisted even through the many layers. Muffled cries of delight at the pleasure, muffled cries of frustration that it wasn't enough.

Shoving a skirt out of the way, reaching up underneath the heavy, draping cloth. Modern underwear easily dealt with, for both of us.

Bent over the piano, feeling it rock against the wheel clamps that kept it from rolling. Would either of us be able to play piano again without thinking of this?

But there was no thought. Only maddening sensations of stroking and probing. Juices smeared, mingling, the sharp scents filling the stuffy room. Everything slick and hot, trembling thighs and thrusting hips.

Wasn't it fine?

The steady rise towards a desperate crescendo, screaming almost soundlessly into the sleeves of our costumes, tearing our throats but not caring, not even thinking about our voices.

Then slinking back to the rehearsal, taking our places on stage after the break as if we'd just gone out to grab a coffee. Certain that everyone knew—but nobody said a word, not then, not ever.

Not even us. We never dared again.

One scene, that's all we have to get through now. We haven't spoken in seven years—why should it be hard to keep silent now?

Isn't it madness, *she* can't be mine?

helpless

HE WAS A wicked, twisted man, and he had her twisted around his little finger. She always had the option of saying no.

She never could.

He knew that.

Music was her release, and he capitalized on that. Fucked her in time to the beat of her favorite songs, but telling her not to come until he said so. The slow songs weren't much easier than the fast ones.

More insidious was the special vibrator that moved and buzzed in time to the music playing through her headphones. Oh, he'd tortured her for a long time with that one.

Unsurprisingly, he wanted more. Wanted to push her farther. And she let him.

She had tickets to her favorite metal band—front and center. Of course she'd dress the part, leather and lace. Nobody would think twice about a collar buckled around her neck.

Except he'd found a new one for her. One with nipple clamps attached. Two chains dangled from the front of the collar, down into her low-cut shirt. Would people know? He assured her, his voice low and threatening, that they would. They'd know just what a slut she was.

And if they didn't, he'd flip up the back of her skirt and show them the stripes where the cane had crashed down, barely redder than the most recent spanking had blushed her round cheeks.

She was surprised when he said she could wear a thong. She shouldn't have been. She shouldn't have seen it as a concession or a gift.

Because before she slipped them up her legs, he pressed a hand against her back, bending her over the bed, her ass in the air. She moaned, afraid and yet craving another assault on her ass.

The fear and arousal had made her wet. His fingers determined that quickly, and he stroked her clit until she was moaning in frustrated arousal.

She almost came when he stuffed the bullet vibrator up into her. She caught herself just in time.

She almost lost it again when she realized what he was going to do. By then it was too late.

They were at the show. The music pounded, and the clamps pulled and pinched as she danced. Her nipples nearly drilled through her top—was it obvious to the band? Probably. She flushed with embarrassment and delight.

He toyed with the remote, playing with the settings. Ratcheting her need to come higher and higher without letting her pitch over the edge. Growling in her ear between songs, describing in exquisite, horrifying detail how she'd be forced to orgasm publicly in front of the entire audience, in front of the band.

She wanted to tell him no.

The music, the humiliation, and the desperate need all screamed *yes*.

As she pitched over the edge, he promised her there was still more to come....

the twelve fucking princesses

ONCE UPON A TIME there were twelve princesses, and every night...

What? Did I *ask* you to stop me if you'd heard this before? Because you might *think* you've heard it, but you don't know the real story. You know the watered-down, sanitized, safe-for-children version.

The truth *really* isn't appropriate for children, trust me.

You really think it's about twelve princesses dancing their shoes to tatters? Have you never heard of euphemisms?

C'mere. Let me tell you what really happened.

Yes, there were twelve princesses, but they weren't sisters, because if they were some of them would be too young for this story. They were at a finishing school, and they were supposed to be sweet virginal things, and the headmaster couldn't figure out where they were sneaking off to every night and half-destroying their clothes.

And smelling suspiciously like certain bodily fluids—both women's and men's.

Not that the headmaster could admit that to their parents, oh no. How could he? He'd get flogged—and not in a way he'd enjoy it. He had to get to the bottom of this before anyone else found out.

He tried locking the door and sitting outside. No go. He tried hiring chaperones to stay in the young women's communal dorm room (because he certainly couldn't), but they all ended up refunding the money and wandering off looking, well, smug. Self-satisfied.

WTF, right?

So word got out about the headmaster's problem—I'm not saying he was advertising, but you know how these things go. And one of the people who heard the word is... let's call him John, shall we? John, not to put too fine a point on it, was an ass. Sure, he wanted the money (by this point, the headmaster was getting a little desperate), but he also figured if he played his cards right, he might get his hands on a little bit of princess treasure, and I'm not talking about gold and jewels.

What do you mean, how do I know all this? Just shut up and let me tell the story.

Okay, I'll wait while you make a joke about pearl necklaces. Let me know when you're done.

John, focused on the allure of money plus potential princess pussy, got the brilliant idea to disguise himself as a woman in order to infiltrate the finishing school and get the currently vacant chaperone job. Normally he would cast aspersions, as they say, on a man dressing in such a fashion, but he told himself it was for the money. And the booty.

Luckily he had a swimmer's build and was blond enough that his body hair wasn't as obvious. A wig and a dress and falsies and heels, and he was there.

Go ahead, snicker. He was an ass. He deserves it.

So, the princesses. Brianna, the eldest, was the de facto leader of the group. Gabrielle was the youngest, and she tended to kowtow to Brianna even though she was pretty sharp herself.

The rest aren't crucial to the story, but because I know you'll ask, their names were Juliana, Simone, Marguerite, Lianne-Marie, Charlotte, Talia, Faris, April, Rosalyn, and Philippa.

Brianna looked at John (who introduced himself as Jonette) and smiled a little smile that would've made him hard if he hadn't tucked his peen back to avoid, er, outing himself.

"I'll be honest," John said. "You know I've been hired not just to give you comportment lessons, but to find out where you're off to every night." He knew saying something that was truthful would disarm them, distract them from his mountain of falsehoods.

"Of course you are," Brianna said. "And you will."

So then it was all about a hidden passageway and crossing an underground lake on a boat (like *that* isn't a metaphor). Gabrielle made sure she was sitting next to Brianna, and she whispered, "Something's not right about Jonette."

"You're a goose," said Brianna. "She's just like all the others."

"Her fashion sense is deplorable, and not in a low-country kind of way," Gabrielle pointed out. "And I just don't like the way she looks at me."

"You won't have to deal with her after tonight," Brianna said. "She'll leave just like all the others."

Brianna never mistreated servants, but she did kind of think they were all the same, interchangeable. Gabrielle sighed and stopped protesting, although she *was* going to say

"I told you so" later because she wasn't perfect and Brianna *was* going to deserve it.

But I'm getting ahead of myself.

John had no idea what he was getting himself in for. Now, I should mention that the fact that the princesses came home each night reeking of various fluids wasn't something the headmaster had shared with *anyone*. If word of *that* got out… Yeah. Not so much.

Given the stories of torn clothing, though, John was expecting some kind of rave, maybe. For all his nasty thoughts, he really didn't have a clue.

They disembarked on a wide, whitewashed dock. Two men came forward and held the boat as the princesses and John jumped out. He trailed behind them into the room so he could keep an eye on them.

Then he was inside, and saw what the princesses were really up to every night.

"Oh, goody." Talia clapped her hands together. "Slave Augustus here. I've been itching to blister his adorable ass."

"And he cries so prettily when you do," Simone said.

"Shall we tag team?"

"Yes, let's!"

They skipped off together, headed for a buff man wearing not much more than some straps cross-crossed around his chest, a posing pouch, and a collar, all made out of burgundy leather.

Swiftly, they tied him down on a spanking bench while another slave gathered implements for them. Because a princess can't mar her pretty, soft white hands, now can she? Talia was rather fond of paddles herself, but Simone chose a flail, and ran her fingers through the strands while she watched her friend go to work on the slave's ass, which was indeed quite adorable, and getting hotter by the moment.

Slave Augustus murmured his thanks after every blow.

Charlotte and Faris had also chosen to share a slave, but to more direct benefit. Charlotte reclined on a feather bed full of pillows while the slave licked her and Faris played with her nipples.

Meanwhile, Rosalyn indulged her slightly subby streak with two men, preparing herself (and them) for an exquisite double penetration. She had a cock in each hand and alternated between sucking them—but skillfully not letting them come just yet.

Subby, yet always in control.

"What's wrong, Jonette?" Brianna asked. "You don't have to be all dom if you don't want to. April and Philippa are as vanilla as they come." She pointed to where each princess was squirming and squealing under the attentive ministrations of an accomplished man whose sole purpose was to give her as many orgasms as possible. "The slaves are just here for our pleasure—you can have them do whatever you want them to do to you."

"Uh, Brianna?" Gabrielle said, because she was starting to figure things out. "I think maybe she—"

"Ohhh!" Brianna said. "Are you a lesbian? There are female slaves here, too." She beckoned to one of the men, who stepped forward, hands clasped behind his back. He was naked except for a short gold chain around his neck.

"No, I…" John panicked.

Then he felt his skirt being pulled up, and before he could react, delicate hands plunged between his legs.

"I *thought* so!" Gabrielle cried. "She's a *man*!"

Something clattered to the floor, and she snatched it up. "And he has a camera," she said. "Spying on us. Probably planning to blackmail our parents."

And then it was too late for John.

The princesses (the ones who hadn't already gotten distracted, that is) pinned him down and, with the help of some of the slaves, had his clothing off, his wrists cuffed to a belt around his waist, and a spreader bar keeping his ankles apart faster than you could say your safeword. He'd've protested, except for the ring gag they slipped into his mouth.

"I think we should let the slaves have some fun for once, don't you?" Brianna asked.

"Excellent idea," Gabrielle agreed, having already thought of it anyway.

Because you know, don't you, that John was very much the type of man to not just be heterosexual and leave it at that. He had an abhorrence of anything that might remotely involve the faintest whiff of homosexuality. (Unless it came to girl-on-girl action, of course. That was entirely different. Charlotte and Faris over there, kissing and fondling each other while Charlotte bounced on the slave's cock and Faris ground herself against his mouth? Hot. Very hot.)

The only thing worse than that? Having anyone he knew suspect *him* of such perversion. Which is why that camera of his came in so damn handy.

They got pictures of him being enthusiastically screwed up the ass by a lucky slave. They got pictures of him wearing a penis gag with an anonymous princess (it was Lianne-Marie, but for obvious reasons her features weren't visible) posting up and down on him—because, of course, the princesses weren't going to let the slaves have *all* the fun. They got pictures of him crying as he was whipped on an X-frame, having his face splashed with come from a circle of slaves, being forced to suck a whole line of men.

Worst of all, they got pictures of him achingly aroused by all of it. His penis straining erect, his balls shaved and bulging around a cock ring. Slaves licking his cock and balls and ass while he writhed and struggled.

A lovely video of him pumping his hips futilely against empty air, ungagged so he could beg to be allowed to come. That was the pièce de la résistance, the ultimate piece of blackmail.

They debated leaving a vibrating butt plug shoved up his sorry ass, but in the end agreed that permanent damage wasn't really necessary. They *did* lock him into a chastity belt and toss the key into the lake on the way back, so he'd have that special added humiliation of asking someone for help removing it.

John slunk off in shame in the middle of the night, never to be heard from again.

And the princesses? Well, let's just say they all went home, got married, and became the power behind the thrones.

Except for Gabrielle. She runs a porn empire. She always did have a head for business.

his lady's manservant

WHEN I CAME into the room with our suitcases, Melina said, "You can put my valise over there."

It wasn't so much what she said, but how she said it: imperious and dismissive in equal measures. She didn't even turn from the dressing table to look at me, as if I was beneath her notice except to do her bidding.

I opened my mouth to point out that we didn't need to be arrived character now, then realized what she was playing at.

My cock stirred.

Oh, you devious woman.

Melina had laughed and laughed when we'd gotten these roles. When you're an out-of-work actor, which we both are, you'll take pretty much anything that'll pay the bills. Playing key roles in a murder mystery weekend scenario at a swanky Victorian B&B would be a nice chunk of change for not a lot of effort.

Except when Melina read the script and discovered that my role was that of a persnickety, detail-oriented butler.

Her role of lady of the manor fit her just fine. Right now she looked stunning, almost otherworldly, in her cream and gold bustle gown, the way her hair piled on her head made her look regal and untouchable and yet incredibly alluring. The only time she ever looked disheveled and out of control was after a particularly rousing bout of sex, which usually involved her wrists being bound to the bedposts or, on occasion, to her thighs.

On the other hand, at home she despaired of my ability to ever pick my dirty socks off the floor or load the dishwasher rather than forgetting bowls and glasses all over the apartment. This part, she'd said, would be quite a stretch for me.

As prideful as I am of my acting abilities, I had to admit she was right.

So far the staging had gone well. In our roles as Lady Clare Morris-Jones and her manservant Mr. J. Burnett, we'd welcomed our "guests" to our "home" and set the stage for the mayhem to follow. Everyone knew the rule that nothing would happen between the hours of 11 p.m. and 8 a.m. That gave us, and the cook (the only other actor) enough rest, and meant the guests could relax as well.

"Thank you, Mr. Burnett," she said. "That will be all. You may go."

Go? What did she—? Oh. Because our roles could have been played by people who didn't know each other, I actually did have a bed in the servant's quarters below stairs.

"You don't mean…"

She finally got up then, and with a rustle of skirts pressed up against me. She set a cool hand against my cheek. "If you play along, I'll make it worth your while tomorrow night," she said,

Her smile was wicked. I hadn't known she'd had it in her. She was always the one wanting to be tied up and teased.

Then again, I'd always been the one wanting to do it. But the way my cock was responding...

I grabbed my shaving kit and headed for the door. Before I walked out, I sketched a submissive bow towards her.

Her laughter followed me down the hallway, and later curled around my cock along with my fingers as I jacked off in anticipation of the next night.

*

It wasn't easy for me, but I finally slipped into the role: running a gloved pinkie over the plate rail to check for dust, picking up empty sherry glasses as soon as they were set down.

But I wasn't perfect, and Melina was always there with a raised eyebrow or a nearly imperceptible shake of her head, if I forgot to hold out a chair for one of the female guests or failed to ask if anyone would like more tea.

Her haughty demeanor was affecting me on several levels. I found myself wanting to please her, to be rewarded by the barest hint of a smile and single nod that said I'd done well.

I also had to find creative ways to keep my cock from tenting my trousers and frightening the guests.

It was a long day.

Finally it ended. Everyone who was supposed to die had kicked the bucket, all the clues were in place, and the final reveal would happen just after breakfast, giving the guests time to get home before nightfall, satisfied with their fun weekend. It was a rare scenario in which the butler *didn't* do it, so my role tomorrow would be minor, just doing butler-ish things. I was thankful for that, because I suspected—hoped— I wouldn't get a lot of sleep tonight.

As long as I'd done my job well today. I always sought to further my craft, but now I had an added incentive: the fear that Melina judged my performance and if she found it wanting, would reject me.

I came to her room with a china cup of warm, honey-dolloped milk on a silver tray.

Her "come" when I knocked made me smile. In my dreams, lady.

"Thank you, Mr. Burnett," she said. I set the tray down, crossed my hands behind my back, waiting for further instruction.

She sipped the milk. "Mr. Burnett," she said again. "I was distressed by your behavior last night. And, if I'm correct, of this afternoon as well."

Holy crap, how had she known? Did she have a spy somewhere? I felt my face redden at the thought.

"Ah, so I was right," she said.

She was just toying with me. She knew me too well. It probably *had* been obvious when I disappeared before dinner. (It was either that, or bring a whole new meaning to the concept of serving the guests.) Or maybe the simple fact that I was growing hard again, right now, in my wool trousers.

"You are here to serve me, are you not?" she asked.

"Yes, ma'am," I said. Melina was taking to this dominance thing far easier than I'd have expected. Then again, she *was* an excellent actress.

I liked it.

"Then come here and help me prepare for bed."

First she instructed me to unpin her hair. While I loosened the fragrant tresses, she went to work on the elbow-length cream-colored gloves, unfastening one button at a time. We're definitely missing out on something major in our less-clothing-is-more modern society; by the time she was peeling the first glove down her arm, I was rock hard.

A second glove gone, and she undid her dress. She stepped out of it with a rustle, and handed it to me to hang up. As much as I wanted to toss it in the corner and get on with things, I did what she wanted, guessing my reward would be worth it.

It was when I was unlacing her corset that it struck me: as I essentially freed her, my actions were binding me to her whims. Not forced bondage by any means—it was entirely by my choice.

She lounged back on the bed, wearing only lace-trimmed bloomers and a matching sleeveless silk camisole and sheer stockings (probably not Victorian-period, but oh, so sexy), and told me to undress.

I shucked my clothes, again wanting to leave them where they fell but instead folding them neatly. Melina's eyes never left me, even as she idly circled one nipple with her finger until the nub blushed dark and hard against the silk.

She was stunning. I wanted to worship her. When she beckoned me to her, I was thrilled that she hadn't found me wanting.

At her command, I suckled her breasts through the silk. The fabric grew damp and see-through, and when I blew on it, she arched her back and mewled with pleasure.

I tugged her drawers down—they were damp, too, with her musky scent—and couldn't resist running the silk across my turgid cock, the fabric excruciatingly soft between my fist and my sensitized flesh.

"We'll have none of that." Melina plucked the bloomers out of my reach. "You're here for my pleasure."

She took my wrists and drew my hands to her breasts, even as she urged my head down between her thighs. With her knees she nudged my legs apart so I was kneeling, not even able to rub my cock against the spread.

Fine. This was her night, her pleasure. I could hope only that if I performed to her satisfaction, I'd get mine as well.

With lips and tongue and fingers I coaxed her higher, higher, until she came in a series of breathy gasps and moans.

Melina tended to be a screamer, and her orgasm solidified our roles: she as the lady of the manor and I as her manservant, the besotted lover kept secret because of class boundaries.

When she rode me (of course she'd take the dominant position), my thoughts truly were for her pleasure. My hands at her breasts, my hips bucking to her rhythm, it wasn't until she was falling over the edge again and gasping "yes, come for me" that I was finally allowed—that I finally allowed myself—the relief I'd craved.

She didn't banish me to the servant's quarters that night, although for the remainder of my roles she stayed in character.

As I loaded our suitcases into the car, I could only think ahead to when we'd reprise our parts…in private.

i need a man

"WHAT'S IT LIKE to fuck a boy?"

Kim and I were lying in a tangle of sweaty limbs and sweaty sheets. I had a bad habit of blurting things out in the post-coital languid daze—usually along the lines of "This isn't working anymore," or, in the case of Kim, "I love you" far earlier than planned.

Kim had gotten used to it since I'd dropped that bomb. But this time, there was more wistfulness in my voice than I'd intended.

"Deciding maybe you're bi after all?" Her voice was light, but she'd stiffened at my words, her body belying her tone.

"Not that I'm aware of." I tried to match my tone to hers. I felt bad for worrying her. I nuzzled her cheek, smelling sex and cherries. "I'm just curious. Really."

Kim had had a few hetero encounters before she realized she was gay. I, on the other hand, had known I was a lesbian by age five, when I was first caught playing doctor with my best friend.

"Boys are…rougher," she said finally. "Your skin is so soft." She ran her hand up my thigh, along the curve of my hip.

I shivered. Maybe I wasn't as sated as I thought.

"Maybe it's their body hair," she mused. "And, somehow, they feel stronger. I've been with big girls, powerful girls, but there's something about a man that feels domineering. Not dominating…just more *there*. Oh, and they're less subtle. It's pretty obvious when they're about to come. With a girl, you have to pay attention to the little signals. The way their breathing changes."

She was right—I inhaled sharply when her teeth grazed my collarbone, then let the air out slowly, through my teeth.

"The way the goosebumps rise on their skin when you touch it."

How did she know my skin would do just that as she trailed her fingers across a new slice of untouched skin?

"The way they quiver, just so, when you stroke…"

Now her hand was between my legs, exploring the fresh wetness, and I stopped caring about differences and subtlety and anything that didn't involve my beautiful and talented girlfriend.

*

I sort of forgot about my question after that. Born in the afterglow, it faded in the reality of daylight and jobs and everyday chores. I suppose a part of me still wondered, but it wasn't keeping me up at night by any stretch.

Kim, on the other hand, has the uncanny ability to squirrel away tidbits of information for later. (She's awesome, for example, when it comes to birthday presents.)

We had a standing Friday night date, sometimes a romantic dinner, sometimes a movie, sometimes a walk on the pier. Tonight it was '80s flashback night at our favorite club.

I got to Club Addiction a little late, but I didn't see Kim's lavender lace headband with the big bow anywhere in sight.

She usually went the Madonna route, all sexy bustier (and who was I to complain?) and fingerless gloves and lots of bracelets. I tended more towards the hair metal look, with zebra-striped Spandex leggings and thigh-high boots.

It didn't really matter. We went there to dance and look at pretty girls.

I ordered a Vodka Sunrise and leaned against the bar to wait for Kim, clinking my fingernail against the glass to the beat of "Don't You Want Me." I smiled hello at a gorgeously androgynous man in a suit à la David Bowie.

No, more like Ultravox, with that slicked-back dark hair and pencil-thin mustache. Warmth pooled in my belly, but from the alcohol. I'd always loved that androgynous look. Annie Lennox at that one awards show had sent me running for my bedroom. But even when it was a male member of a New Romantics group, I'd still felt a frisson of desire—because what if that slender, effeminate guy turned out to be a woman after all, down underneath that natty, light grey suit?

What if?

I'm embarrassed to say how long it took me to recognize Kim. I politely rejected "his" advances more than once before I heard Kim's husky timbre beneath what I finally noticed was a falsely lowered voice, before I caught Kim's habit of tracing circles against the side of her glass with her forefinger.

Before I saw the oh-so familiar glint of amusement and lust in her blue eyes.

"Want to dance?" she asked again, and this time, I agreed.

Usually we went to the club to bop around to the bouncier songs, but Cyndi Lauper's "Time After Time" seemed perfect right now.

Kim had done a great job, I had to say, right down to using a men's aftershave rather that her usual perfume. But when we went cheek-to-cheek on the dance floor, I caught the underlying scent that was so very *her*.

My nipples hardened under my ripped Mötley Crüe T-shirt. I hadn't figured it out, but Kim had put it all together, and dug out my ultimate fantasy. I didn't want a boy, not really. I wanted to *pretend* I was with a pretty boy.

The fact that it was someone I loved made it even better.

Then she flexed her hips, and I felt her other surprise pressing against my mound.

"Well, *hel*lo," I said.

She laughed and nipped my earlobe. "Special present, just for you," she whispered. She slid her hands around my hips and pulled me close, grinding the fake erection against me.

The room spun. Or maybe it was just me, spinning on the heady lust of being in the arms of my girlfriend, who'd dressed like a man to tap into my darkest dreams, a fake cock nudging against my crotch. The promise of sex later, or, if we weren't careful, some serious pleasure right here on the dance floor, in front of everyone.

You can't wear panties under Spandex. Not even a thong. So the fact was, I knew immediately just how wet I was getting, and given a little more time, when we pulled apart, the rest of the bar would know, too.

"Come home with me?" Kim growled in my ear, still in persona. She punctuated the words with a series of thrusts, and if the question had taken longer, I would've climaxed right there.

"I'll follow you," I said.

Because at that moment, I would've followed her anywhere.

*

A passionate kiss in the driveway, pressing me up against my car while she groped under my T-shirt. Through the house to the bedroom, her hand on my ass, not pausing to check the mail or top off the cat's water bowl.

There was no question in my mind what I needed to do next.

On my knees, I parted the crotch of her pants and drew out her cock. (Her cock, his cock, it didn't matter anymore. I was lost in the fantasy, stunned by the reality.)

She'd found as realistic a dildo as I could imagine (having not spent any quality time with a hard prick in my life, and pictures aren't the same). The way it jutted out from between her thighs, I could believe she was a man.

Wrapping my lips around the hard rod and smearing my lipstick down it made my nipples so hard, they hurt.

"That's it, baby, suck me." Kim's eyes were half-lidded as she watched me. "You suck it so good."

She stripped off the jacket, but left on the T-shirt beneath. She had smallish, beautifully rounded breasts, but she must have been wearing a sports bra, because her chest looked flat, adding to the male visage. I moaned around my mouthful.

"You want more, don't you?"

Of course I did. Stupid question. I sat back on my heels and watched her slip off the loafers, kick away the pants. She left the T-shirt on.

We'd never used a harness before, previously content to play with dildos and vibrators and our hands. She wore a pair of men's tightie-whities, concealing the straps beneath. The sight of the fake cock springing from her crotch through the fly thrilled me.

She tugged me to my feet, led me to the bed. I started to lie back, but she shook her head and positioned me on my hands and knees. Of course. This way I could still fantasize, pretend to whatever degree I wanted and needed that she was a he.

I was wet, oh, so wet, but she felt me first with her hand, probing between my lips and then, as I watched over my shoulder, spreading it on the tip of the cock.

Stroking it like a man would.

I shuddered.

Just before she touched me again, Kim tapped the iPod on the night table.

Annie Lennox wailed the chorus of "I Need a Man."

My pussy clenched, a barely there mini-orgasm. Not enough, not nearly enough, but I was astonished nonetheless.

I wanted more. Needed more. If Kim didn't fuck me soon, I might go out of my mind.

She pressed the cock between my lips, rubbing it up and down, hissing as it skidded in my wetness. I imagined that was the best feeling for a man, touching that wet warmth, anticipating being surrounded by it. When she brushed against my clit, I wiggled back, eager for more pressure.

But she slipped away, teasing at my entrance, moving in time with my hips so I couldn't get her to sink in any deeper, either.

Why was she tormenting me so?

Then it hit me.

"Fuck me," I said. The words didn't come easily, but once they left my mouth, there was no stopping them. "Fuck me, please. Fuck me with your big hard—"

The rest was lost in a gulp of air as she did exactly what I begged for.

I'd had dildos inside of me before, so I didn't expect it to be different or new. I couldn't have been more wrong. This was entirely different. Maybe it was the buildup, maybe it was the vision of Kim in that suit dancing behind my closed eyes. Maybe it was the music, and the memory of those tightie-whities with a stiff cock thrusting out, eager for my mouth.

It was all of that, and more. It was the way her hands gripped my hips, her fingers digging in almost painfully. It was the soft grunts she made, a sound I'd never heard before.

It was the way she moved, so unlike her normal motion.

Kim's thighs weren't rough like a man's might have been, but her strokes were strong, demanding. Because she used her thighs rather than her hand to drive the cock into me? Didn't know, didn't care.

I reached between my legs, felt the slick rod stretching my lips open, devoured and devouring.

"That's it, baby," she moaned. "Come for me." She'd abandoned all pretense of the lower voice, and the knowledge that she was on the edge, too, was more than enough for me.

I stroked my clit, and as I did, her thrusts changed, short and staccato, and I knew she was coming, too. That's all I knew, because I was thrusting back, burying the dildo in me, and I was coming apart, shattering and reforming around the touch of her hands. The sound of her harsh cries brought me to another orgasm and back to earth, grounded again.

We collapsed together, dildo still lodged inside me.

"I love you," I said, and it wasn't one of those post-coital slips.

As she already knew, it was true.

invitation to a spanking

JILL BENT OVER the bed, palms flat by her face, her right cheek resting on the purple-and-gold brocade spread. Her eyes were closed, but already she had a beatific smile on her pretty face.

It was her ass I was more interested in, though. Mildly obsessed with, you could say.

High, heart-shaped, and firm, slendering down to thighs toned by bike riding. A hint of dark, trimmed pubic hair peeking out. Best of all, a constellation of freckles dusted her smooth flesh. I don't know why that aroused me so much, just that it did. Mm, yes, it did.

Oh, how my hand tingled, anticipating the first smack just as much as she did. The feel of that skin against mine, the resultant jiggle, the way the imprint would bloom.

I tortured us both by delaying. I glanced at her husband, but his gaze was also riveted on her inviting cheeks.

I raised my hand....

*

It started with a personal ad.

Happily married couple seeking female spanking aficionado to warm wife's bottom. No sex involved.

That made me sit up straighter in the hard wooden coffee shop seat—and squirm a little, too. I love giving a firm, hard spanking. I can't say I dislike getting my own ass blistered from time to time, but doing the spanking myself? I imagine it's like how an opera singer feels performing a perfect aria: Soaring.

My heart beating just a little harder, I took a sip of my steaming cappuccino and scanned the ad again. It could be a bunch of crock—personals in the city weekly paper often are—but something about it spoke to me. Sent me tingling all over, including the good places.

It felt right in my gut…and below.

So I made contact, they responded, and we arranged a meeting the next day.

My pussy hummed as I waited in the park, admiring the pretty red and white flowers spilling from the baskets that hung from the faux-antique light posts.

An attractive couple pedaled up on bicycles and dismounted a few feet away. The woman approached me.

"Shar?" she asked with a hint of hesitance.

"Sharon, actually," I said, rising and shaking her hand. I hadn't used my full name, either, in case this were some sort of scam.

To my growing delight, it didn't look like a scam at all. They introduced themselves as Jill Tomita and Christopher Carlisle. They were, like me, in their early forties. While they didn't seem to be gym rats, they were clearly active and fit. She was Asian American, with straight black hair and a smattering of freckles on her nose and high cheekbones. He had dirty blond hair cropped close and warm brown eyes.

Time to get down to business. I asked, and they answered.

Jill wanted to be spanked. Christopher was hesitant. He'd read about it, but still felt unsure. He'd been ingrained with the concept that you didn't strike a woman—not a bad tenet overall, really. Just not one that meshed when the woman in question craved having her bottom blistered.

So they'd come up with the idea that if he saw Jill enjoying a proper spanking, it would help break down his barriers. They'd both agreed that they'd be more comfortable with a woman doing the deed. Jill was nominally bi: she'd had the obligatory college experiences, but was monogamous in her marriage.

Of course, sex itself wasn't in the agreement—at least, not between them and me. What they did after I left was up to them.

So then I asked to speak to each of them individually, to be extra sure they were both doing this for the right reasons; that neither had talked the other into it.

Christopher went first. I ogled Jill as she walked away. Her ass really was perfect. She wasn't so skinny that her thighs didn't touch. I mean, where's the fun in that? For a spanking, you've got to have some juicy flesh.

I noticed Christopher watching, too. A good sign.

"'Fess up," I said. "What's the real reason you don't want to spank her?"

He looked down at his hands. They were broad, capable, solid. Perfect for caressing, holding…and spanking, absolutely. I sometimes get crushes on men just from their hands. Jill was going to be a lucky woman, provided this little plan worked.

He reiterated what he'd said before, about not wanting to hit a woman. I waited. I knew there was more.

Finally he said, "I know it's what she wants, and I'd give her the world if I could. I just…I don't want to do it wrong, you know?"

Aw. That was just adorable. I patted his arm.

"Don't worry. I'll give you pointers…and afterwards, I'm sure Jill will let you know what she likes."

Jill was even more forthcoming. There was no question that this is absolutely what she wanted—craved, even.

It was clear they loved each other, that they both wanted this to happen, but they didn't know how to do that. They need a fulcrum, a catalyst, an instigator.

They needed me.

*

That's how it started, and now I was here—we were here—and the world narrowed to my raised hand and Jill's waiting ass. Christopher was silent; I think he was holding his breath. I think we all were.

As if apart from myself, I saw my hand flash through the air, nails painted OPI Diva of Geneva hot pink. Felt the sting against my palm as I connected with her ass. Saw the judder of flesh, the rise of rosy blush.

My own cheeks clenched, savoring the memory of what that sensuous blow felt like.

I caressed the pert globes of her ass, petting away the sting. Preparing her for the next flash of delicate pain.

The scent of her arousal tickled my nose, hot and musk and spices. My own panties—I'd worn lavender lace with a bouquet of tiny flowers in the front, even though nobody but me would see them—were damp with desire.

I struck her again, glorying in the sensation and in the sound of her tiny gasp.

This wasn't about hardcore BDSM. This wasn't about whips and chains and dungeons. It wasn't, really about bondage at all: Jill's hands were flat on the bed, although her fingers twitched, and I guessed she wanted to reach down, explore the wetness created by nothing more than the throbbing of her spanked, hot flesh. If she caressed her swollen clit, she'd probably come in no time.

But she didn't. This was about pain and pleasure and arousal and need and…not quite denial, no. Anticipation. A hint of submission.

Mostly, though, the smarting ache of her flesh and the feel of my hand connecting with it again and again.

Throughout the scenario, I'd been explaining to Christopher what I was doing and why. How the flesh of the upper thigh, just beneath the curve of the ass, is especially tender. How each strike has to be controlled but confident. Trust yourself. Trust your partner.

A whimper escaped her, and my clit twitched. I liked it when pretty women reacted to what I did to them.

She was almost ready. She rolled her hips, and I rolled mine, as slick and wet and needy as if I'd been the one receiving the spanking.

We'd set out a paddle and a soft red suede flogger. Nothing too hardcore; if they decided to try a cane or a whip, that would come later. But honestly, right now, the paddle and flogger were superfluous. My desire was hand on flesh, and clearly Jill's was the same.

I spanked her again, delighting in the feel, the sound, the scent. And as I did, I tipped my head at Christopher.

In a flash he was on his feet. I stepped aside to let him take my place. Jill's eyes were closed, a faint glisten of tears on her cheek and a faint smile on her lips. She didn't know what would come next, but I suspect she knew it would be better than what came before, if only because that's the way the evening had gone so far.

Christopher raised his hand, looked at me. Beneath his hesitation, he was as ready as Jill. He just needed to believe. I nodded.

His hand, his perfect broad hand, connected smartly with Jill's ass, exactly right.

There was a brief moment when she froze, and then I saw her body shudder and crack beneath the force of an orgasm she didn't expect. Her eyes flew open, but unseeing; her mouth formed an O as she keened, high and stunned and overwhelmed by the force of it.

It was all I could do to stumble out of their bedroom, pulling the door shut behind me before I half-collapsed against the wall, the shimmerfall of something akin to an orgasm turning my thighs to delicious mush.

As I staggered my way out their front door, fumbling for my keys, I realized how reading that personal ad had changed their lives.

Now I was off to find a sweet young thing who craved a spanking—or maybe a sweet young to focus on my tender bottom.

> *Female spanking aficionado looking to warm your
> wife's or girlfriend's bottom. No sex involved….*

just be

I WAS CONVINCED Sarita was going to leave me.

The hushed phone calls, hanging up when I came into the room.

The fact that we hadn't had sex in over a month, and over a month before that, and probably more but I'd blocked it out. And even those had been rushed.

The suitcase I found in her closet yesterday morning when I was looking for a scarf I thought she'd borrowed, although she hadn't mentioned any trips to me.

But it had all probably started before that. The night I was late to her birthday dinner, rushing into the restaurant from a study session that had run long, and her looking up from the table, her luminous brown eyes glowing disappointment in the candle flame even as everyone at the table fell silent for a moment.

We'd known my going to law school would be a burden on us both. At the time, we'd made the decision together, discussed the potential problems, worked out solutions. I'd gotten scholarships so money wouldn't be a big issue; I'd be too busy to spend frivolously anyway. We'd have to cut back on traveling, but there would be summers. That sort of thing.

Going back to school, especially this kind of intense studying, was harder than I expected. I guess when you're thirty you don't have the kind of resilience you do in your late teens and early twenties. You don't have the momentum of coming out of high school straight into college, or cannon-shot from college into grad school.

Sarita and I barely saw each other, and when we did, my head was spinning with torts and USC sections, and I was rambling about fellow students whom she'd never met.

And the screeching halt in our sex lives, well. Nobody would have expected us, with our reputation of being screwing-like-bunny dykes, to be falling asleep with no more than a brush of a kiss and a snuggle.

Every damn night.

I'd abandoned her, and she was probably just being her usual wonderful self by waiting until after my stress-crazy finals to tell me that it was over.

I don't know how I made it through finals. I remember waiting to be handed the Constitutional Law test, on the verge of tears from thinking about my life empty without her, and then the paper was in front of me and my world narrowed to articles and amendments.

Hours later, I looked up, and my stomach twisted again. You'd think I'd feel relief that finals were over. Instead, I was sure they spelled the beginning of the end.

I grabbed a Snickers bar from the vending machine—I didn't remember eating breakfast, and I'd skipped lunch in favor of some last-minute cramming—and headed to my car.

Sarita was standing by it. My steps slowed even as my body tingled. With her dark East Asian complexion, she could pull off fire-engine red like nobody's business. The little stretch lace tank top hugged her high breasts. She'd paired it with khaki shorts and a pair of red thong sandals.

Her toenails were the same shade of red as her shirt. Sexy right down to the details.

Did she have to look so good just to dump me?

"Hey," she said when I got close, and stepped forward into a kiss.

Out of familiar habit and familiar desire, I responded, letting myself focus on nothing more than the feel of her soft mouth moving against mine, her teeth gently nipping my bottom lip before she stepped back.

"Will your car be okay here over the weekend?" she asked.

Confused, I nodded. The student lot was open 24/7.

"Good. You're coming with me."

I followed her, too brain-fogged to form a coherent question. She asked about the tests, and I told her how I thought I'd done (Contracts, pretty well; Criminal Law, hard to say). It wasn't until we pulled onto the freeway in the opposite direction from home that I had the foresight to ask, "Where are we going?"

"Yosemite," Sarita said, flashing me a grin.

That was entirely beyond my current comprehension level.

"You need a break, sweetheart," she said. Her hand on my knee wasn't helping, but I tried really hard to concentrate on her words. "You've been studying your ass off, and now finals are over and you deserve a vacation. We both do. You get to decompress and we get to re-acquaint ourselves with each other."

I took her hand from my leg and pressed my mouth against her palm. It was the only way I could express my gratitude and relief.

And then I did something I wouldn't've thought possible.

I fell asleep.

I stayed asleep until we were pulling up to the ranger station to pay our entrance fee, bleary and blinking and needing to pee.

I apologized to Sarita for not helping with the driving, but she waved my contrition away.

"You were exhausted," she said. "I'm glad you were able to sleep. It means you're starting to relax and let go."

We stopped to stretch and pick up a few last-minute supplies and change into hiking gear, then continued on into the park. Apparently Sarita had thought of everything, including packing all the stuff I'd need. That explained the suitcase in the closet, and the phone calls.

Despite my nap, I still felt groggy and overwhelmed, like I was dizzy and wandering around in a fog. Strapping on the packs and hiking up to the meadow went a long way to clearing that fog. We didn't speak much, just occasionally to point out an eagle overhead or to comment in awe over the views. All of Yosemite looks like a postcard, a surreal, impossible beauty.

Kind of like Sarita. Dazed and confused as I was, as the hike progressed and the weight and stress of school peeled away, feelings I thought I'd lost resurfaced: Arousal. Desire. Lust.

It wasn't just the brisk air that quickened my breath and hardened my nipples. Oh no. Watching Sarita's lithe form moving gracefully up the path was doing wonders for my formerly buried libido.

The sun was no more than a blushing glow behind Half Dome by the time we had the tent set up and the fire going. Since it was late, supper was simple: canned stew, fresh sourdough bread, and cherries for dessert.

In the flickering firelight, I watched the cherries stain Sarita's lush lips a deeper red, and I quivered right down to my clit.

She looked up, saw me watching her. Must have seen the look in my eyes, because she smiled, tossed the pit in the fire, and leaned over to kiss me.

Like the kiss at the car, it was slow, gentle, gradually deepening. Dimly, I realized that I understood the cliché of air to a drowning man. I breathed in the feel of Sarita against me and felt alive again.

The skin of her bare arms was satiny under my hands. Suddenly I wanted to be naked, feel my body against hers: soft belly, hard hipbones, sharp nipples, silken hair above and coarse below. I wanted it so badly that my hands shook.

"You taste so good," Sarita whispered, licking the hollow of my breastbone. "I've missed the taste of you."

"I've missed you, too. I'm so sorry—"

She pressed her lips against mine again until she was sure I'd stopped trying to talk, then said, "Ssh. Don't talk. Just be."

I let tears of wonder drain back into my throat and kissed her, cupping her beautiful face in my hands. Her tongue darted in and out of my mouth, teasing and playful, and my pussy contracted as I thought about how that teasing touch would feel on my clit.

We tumbled back onto the sleeping bag we'd cleverly laid out already. Sarita knelt over me, unbuttoning my shirt and leaving trailing kisses along the exposed skin, then deftly undoing the front hook of my bra. Cool air slid over me before she took my breasts in her hand and warmed first one, then the other nipple with her wet mouth.

It had been so long since we'd touched that my cunt ached from the sudden rush and swell of desire.

I think we might both have had it in our heads to take this slow, to savor and celebrate. Our bodies, however, had other plans.

I reached up to brush my palms across her breasts. She was braless beneath the tank top, and her nipples distended the fabric. She hissed as I pinched, first gently, then harder. Her hips twitched, which pressed her crotch harder against mine.

"Sarita!"

It wasn't quite an orgasm, or maybe you could call it a mini-orgasm. I know I shuddered with pleasure, cried out her name. Whatever it was, it was enough for her to expertly strip me of my shorts and part my thighs with her long-fingered hands.

Then her mouth was on me, and she licked and sucked my swollen clit, and that was enough to send me off on a real orgasm, one incredibly long one or maybe a string of them.

She kissed me, her face covered in my juices, and moments later I was between her legs and returning the favor, two fingers stroking her deep inside as I licked her until she screamed.

After that we slowed down, stroking and whispering and luxuriating in having all the time in the world to make love.

Sometime after *that*, with a waxing moon high in the sky and stars like you've never seen, we threw half the sleeping bag over us and finally talked.

I admitted I'd thought she was leaving me. She was shocked, protesting until I kissed her quiet just as she had done to me earlier.

"The look you gave me when I was late to your birthday dinner…"

"I was worried about you," she said. "You'd been working so hard and not eating, and you walked in and you looked so pale and gaunt… I wanted everyone else to go away so I could feed you and take you home and put you to bed."

"I'm sorry things got so crazy," I said.

"I'm sorry I couldn't do anything to make it easier," she said.

Then we both laughed, because we knew we were being silly apologizing for things we couldn't control.

We'd find a way to work it out. Communicate better, take the occasional weekend or even just a day or an evening to reconnect during the most stressful times.

As the embers pulsed orange and hot in the fire ring, I looked up and watched a bat swoop overhead.

And just let myself *be*.

obey all signs

"DURING YOUR DRIVING TEST, the examiner will note how you obey the rules of the road and traffic signs and/or signals," Chuck quoted from the DMV handbook.

I stared, dumbfounded, at the road sign, then at my husband. "Are you *serious*?"

"You want to pass the test, don't you?" His voice was stern, his expression implacable.

My rational brain panicked, while at the same time my body betrayed me, my panties flooding with moisture and my nipples springing to attention so suddenly that the seatbelt, rubbing against one, was excruciating.

I'd grown up in the city, never needing a car until we'd married and moved to California where public transportation was a joke. Chuck was coaching me. I'd been doing fine so far—not running through yellow lights, looking both ways at intersections, remembering my turn signal when I changed lanes.

"It's not a verb, like Stop," I protested. "It's a noun, like Railroad Crossing."

"Do you think arguing with the driving examiner is going to help you pass?" Chuck asked.

Of course not. More importantly, arguing with Chuck always got me into more trouble. In deliciously perverse ways.

Like right now. He'd had me drive his convertible to a fairly remote road and instructed me to pull over just before the caution sign that said, simply, "Hump."

And he wanted me to obey that sign.

Knowing I had a hang-up about public sex.

Weak thighs and a fluttering stomach joined my growing symptoms of arousal. That explained why he'd had me wear a pencil skirt with a thigh-high slit: Not to turn on the faceless examiner I hadn't yet met, but for Chuck himself. And for me, because I could hike it over my hips.

I did that now.

"Give me your panties," Chuck said.

Cheeks flaming, I couldn't keep from glancing around to make sure no other cars had crept up while I wasn't looking. Wriggling out of my underwear in the confined space took a little doing, but eventually I managed.

A wicked glint in Chuck's dark eyes. "Sopping," he said, approval in his voice, before he hung them over the rearview mirror, filling the air with my musk.

He told me to spread my legs, stroke myself until I was close, ease off, do it again. I hated that, hated being denied, loved that he could make me even though I hated it. Truth was, I didn't come very close. I was constantly aware of where we were, outside, public, with the chance of anyone driving down that road at any moment.

Then, finally, he opened his pants, freeing his fat cock, and I clambered over to straddle him, sink down with a delighted shudder. He unbuttoned the top of my shirt so he could reach in, tweak my nipples.

I posted, ground down, *humped*. I didn't whimper like I usually did, out of desire and frustration and lust. No, I practically held my breath, listening. And then, ohgodohgod, I heard the whine of an engine, a motorcycle, growing louder.

Closer.

"Someone's coming," I whispered frantically. No idea why I felt the need to whisper. Just panic.

"Well, then," Chuck said, "you'd better come pretty fast, because you don't get to stop until you do."

I couldn't, but I had to, and the frantic terror of being caught wove together with frustrated need, the need to come, building higher and higher until I was sure the bike was just around the corner and something snapped inside of me and I came, shrieking and shuddering in a red-wash of hot sunlight.

At the same time, I felt Chuck's cock swell, and his hips slammed up, prolonging my orgasm with his own.

"Get back in your seat," Chuck hissed, and somehow I managed to, with my skirt pulled down again, as the motorcycle approached behind us. I could feel Chuck's come trickling out of me as I tried, and probably failed, to look nonchalant.

The motorcyclist slowed down, way down, and for a moment of sheer dread I wondered if this were a further plan of Chuck's—not that my orgasm-addled brain could figure out what traffic law could be interpreted to mean sucking off a stranger. Then I realized he was looking at my flushed cheeks, my half-open shirt…and my panties dangling in full view from the mirror.

And as he gunned the motor to speed away, that realization sent my traitorous body into another shaking orgasm.

subtle

KARINA AND I have never been into hard-core bondage. The idea of thick straps of leather everywhere, of crosses and horses and all-out full-on immobility just doesn't do it for us.

No, we're much more subtle than that. Believe me, the results are just as, if not more, devastating.

It started one night when we were playing with nipple clamps. We were using light, teasing ones, because let's face it, your hands can't be everywhere, and what's wrong with a little help?

Karina got a deliciously evil look on her face. At that point, I hadn't quite learned just what that look meant. I shivered nonetheless; I instinctively knew that it was a good thing.

We were in the front hall next to the stairs. We'd been romping in the living room and had decided to head for the bedroom.

We never made it.

Karina got that wicked gleam in her eyes. She slid one of the padded tweezer clips off my pouting nipple, threaded the attached chain through a railing on the banister, and reattached the clamp.

"Stay there," she said, and bounded up the stairs.

There was no danger, obviously. My hands and feet were free. I could have popped off one of the clips and gone on my merry way.

But I didn't. I don't think I could have. Even though logically I knew there was nothing physical truly holding me there, mentally it was clear: I was stuck. She'd told me to stay. Stay I would.

The realization made me squirm. My nipples swelled, throbbing in the clips. As I shifted, I could tell my pussy lips were slick, pouting. How long would she leave me like this?

When Karina came down the stairs with a bright blue fake cock jutting from her groin, my head spun.

She stopped, crouched, slid the dildo through the railings. I took it in my mouth. She'd used it on herself first—I could taste her arousal. My moan was muffled.

She pulled away, came the rest of the way down, and fucked me hard from behind. Gripping the railings, thrusting my ass back to meet her strokes, I was constantly aware of the chain hanging loosely between the bars.

That's what pushed me over the edge, again and again.

*

So that's how it began. It was always the subtle stuff: a pair of thumbscrews so I couldn't pull my hands apart, a pair of strappy high heels that locked together. She tied my calves to the dining room chair legs with silken cords so I had to concentrate on my dinner and try to ignore the fact that my uncovered cunt was spread and dripping.

It didn't help when Karina suggested we do something similar at a restaurant, under a long tablecloth.

She let me loose long enough so we could go upstairs, where she tied my legs to the bedposts with the same cords and teased me with a vibrator on my clit to the peak of orgasm while I vainly tried to pull my thighs together.

*

We have an iron bedstead, with a low footboard that's flush with the mattress. She bent me over the bed, as we'd done a hundred times before. She had the strap-on buckled around her slim hips again.

This time, though, the stakes were raised. The nipples clamps were threaded through the footboard, so every time she thrust into me, they tugged at my nipples. Not hardcore pain, but a mind-bogglingly strong sensation nonetheless. I tried to squirm backwards, but a firm hand on the small of my back stopped me.

Once again, my hands were free. I could've stopped things at any time.

But I didn't want to.

Thrust. Tug. Thrust. Tug. Until it was all a blur, and then I was shaking and crying out, my inner walls clamping down on the dildo and my hands fisted in the bedspread as I came.

*

Karina gradually grew more inventive, more devious.

Take tonight, for instance.

We had a gallery opening to go to. She told me I'd particularly enjoy it. Silly me, I thought she meant the art.

She strapped narrow cuffs (black leather with little red hearts on them) around my thighs and buckled them together. I could walk, certainly, but only in short, mincing steps. A simple thing that had a devastating effect on me.

Before she did that, though, she had me spread my legs wide (which I wouldn't be able to do for a while) and inserted a series of three metal balls, connected by a cord, deep up inside me. The balls were weighted, so when I walked (even with those tiny steps), they jiggled and rocked, a constant reminder of my sexy predicament.

Finally, there were tiny little rings that bit into my already-hard nipples. Every time I took a breath, I felt them.

I wore a long skirt and a loose blouse, elegant and striking. The items that teased me and tormented me wouldn't be obvious to anyone else. There was nothing to indicate I wasn't just having an ordinary evening out with my lover, enjoying fine art.

Subtle. Wicked.

If a friend of ours wasn't the artist having the show, I would have begged to stay home. At the same time, the long, slow arousal of the evening would mean an explosive time after we returned home. I wondered if she had more in store for me then.

The gallery was divided into two main areas, one a few steps lower than the other, connected by wide, shallow steps. People tended to gather on the stairs, chatting, and we were no different. So I was completely unprepared when I heard a tiny *snick*, and realized that Karina had snapped a chain onto the bracelet on my left wrist, and then to the railing. At the same time, she'd draped my wrap over my arm, so it simply looked as though I was standing there, casually resting my hand on the railing.

I was trapped.

She stepped a few feet away to greet someone we knew, and I wondered how long she would leave me there. And to what end?

The conversation ebbed and flowed, rising and falling around me, and over it all the strains of jazz wailed softly from hidden speakers. Friends paused to talk, to discuss the artwork and find out how we'd been doing.

Okay. I could handle this. I was horny as hell, shivering a little from the way my nipples had gotten rock hard and aching, how my clit throbbed. But it was all mind games, right? Nothing I could deal—

That's when I found out that the balls in my pussy vibrated, and she had the remote control.

Luckily nobody was standing next to me at the precise moment the evil orbs started humming of their own accord. I muted my gasp into a delicate cough, and pressed my lips together so I wouldn't moan. My hand clenched around the railing.

The glass of champagne in my other hand wobbled dangerously.

I looked around frantically. There wasn't a waiter to be seen. I didn't think I could reach the floor to set the crystal flute down, much less do it in a way that didn't look odd.

I was too aroused to even gulp what was left in the glass.

Oh, she had me. She had me good. I knew that all I had to do was call out to her, and she'd stop the torture. But calling out to her would also look a little odd, and she knew I hated to look gauche in public.

I was truly at her tender mercies.

Sweat broke out on my upper lip. I tried to spread my legs, minimize the exquisite torture, but of course I couldn't, thanks to the cuffs.

Pressing my thighs together was a far worse idea. It made everything more intense, reminded me that my clit was swollen and sensitive. My inner walls jumped as I tried to stave off the inevitable, and it seemed that the vibrations increased.

I sent a panicked glance at Karina. She smiled and blew me a kiss, as if that's all it was, lovers connecting across a crowded room.

The vibrations *had* increased, and she was the one making it happen.

My entire body was one big throbbing mass of sensation, from breasts to groin, nipples to clit. I was sure if someone touched my bare arm, I'd come. I was terrified that someone would.

At any point, I could have stopped it. Somewhere, deep in the back of my brain, I knew that. It would be easy enough to undo the chain at my wrist, scurry to the bathroom and remove the cuffs and the torturous spheres. Or, with a simple signal from me, Karina would turn off the vibrating balls that seemed to have expanded inside me, stretching me as they rocked and pulsed.

I knew it, but I didn't know it. All I really knew was that Karina had me trapped, and she was going to play with me, both physically with the toys and mentally by smiling sweetly at me, until I came.

Came in public, in a roomful of people.

The only question was how long it would take.

My entire body tightens. The familiar surge, like a growing wave, swells within me. This time, I can't stop it.

Oh God…

working late

JACK HAD TO work late again, on a Friday, no less.

Rain sluiced down the windows, the drops and streams sparkling in the gleam of passing headlights. A dreary night. I slipped my wireless headphone over my ear and dialed my husband's number. As I waited for him to pick up, I clicked the icon on my computer to link with his webcam.

I saw Jack's face and heard his voice at the same time. His dark brown hair was mussed; he'd probably been running his fingers through it in frustration. He needed a haircut, too, poor thing.

"Hello, darling," I said. "How's it going?"

"Just finishing up," he said, closing a folder on his desk.

I glanced at my watch. "Good. Just in time."

The tone of my voice had changed with those last words, clear to him even over the phone. He sat taller in his chair, and his grey eyes briefly unfocused. "Yes, ma'am," he said.

I don't think he'd realized how late it was until I mentioned it. He easily got lost in his work.

"Close your office door."

He briefly left my field of vision. When he sat back down, I asked, "Is anyone else still at work?"

"I don't think so."

His office had a window to the corridor, but the way his desk was situated, he was mostly blocked from outside view by his 30-inch flat panel Apple Cinema Display monitor. Still, better to be safe than sorry.

I reached for my glass of Scotch, sipped. Ice tinkled in the tumbler as I set it back down.

"Get the package I put in your briefcase this morning," I instructed. "Make sure you bring it back in front of the camera."

Well-trained, he didn't open the black velvet drawstring bag, just sat back down and waited.

Jack enjoyed our games just as much as I did.

"Remove the items."

His chest heaved when he saw what I'd packed for him. What I had planned for him.

"Tell me what you've found."

He tried to speak, failed, cleared his throat, and started again. "A pair of small clamp—nipple clamps. A butt plug, and a packet of lube. Ma'am."

"Tell me what you're going to do with them."

Sometimes I gave orders, but often Jack was smart enough to know what I wanted. I mean, duh, they weren't unusual toys. Besides, having him describe what was going to happen heightened the anticipation—for both of us.

My breasts felt heavy, swollen beneath my silk blouse. I didn't need to look to know my own nipples were clear against the soft fabric.

"I'm going to go to the men's room and put the clamps on my nipples. I'll probably have to massage my nipples a little to get them ready for the clamps." Jack looked down at the items on his desk. "I'll coat the plug with lube, and also my fingers, and open myself up before inserting the plug."

"Will you like that?"

It wasn't an easy question and didn't have an easy answer. He had a love-hate relationship with the plug, craved the sensation while aware of how it looked, what it meant.

"Yes, ma'am," he said.

"Then what?"

"I'll come back to my desk, and when you see me, you'll call me with further instructions."

"Good boy. Go on, then."

He vanished from the screen. I leaned back in my leather chair, propped one stocking-clad foot on a half-open file drawer. (I'd kicked off my shoes somewhere beneath the desk ages ago.) His steps would be a little heavy, I knew, but he wouldn't dawdle. He knew he'd be in trouble if he didn't get back to his desk in a certain amount of time. (If he did run in to a co-worker, he would tell me, and that would let him off the hook.)

Beneath my skirt, my stretch lace panties were damp. I ran my fingertips lightly over the crotch, smelling my pungent musk. I indulged in a little over-the-fabric petting, enjoying the tease as I imagined what Jack was doing.

The nipple clamps were light ones, just enough to give a little pinch and keep him aware of his chest. They were small enough that they wouldn't be obvious beneath his crisp eggplant-hued shirt.

He'd stand in the stall with one foot on the toilet, one hand braced against the wall as he gently stretched his own ass with one, then two fingers. The sheen of a light sweat would break out on his brow when he angled the plug and rocked it in and out, readying himself further. When it popped in, his eyes would close. A moment of adjustment, his body rigid, and then he'd sigh ever so slightly.

After that there was the matter of stuffing his hardening cock back into his pants. I felt a bit of sympathy for him there. We women just didn't have to contend with that problem.

The plug would be heavy inside him and the clamps would cause a faint throb in his sensitive nubs as he walked back to his office.

I sat upright, both feet on the floor, when he came back into view. He sat down gently, settling himself into the chair as if he didn't really want to come into contact with the seat.

I was tempted to tell him to drop trou and prove he'd inserted the plug, but given the risk of being caught, I didn't. Besides, I *did* trust him.

It just would've been fun to see his face when I suggested it.

"How're you feeling?" I asked cheerfully when he answered the phone.

"Stuffed full, ma'am," he answered. "Thank you."

I couldn't keep the smile off my face. "Are you turned on, Jack?" I asked, my voice low. "Is that plug knocking against your prostate? Do you like feeling full? Is your cock hard?"

The questions were making me hot, that was for sure. My nipples throbbed in time with my clit. Turning him on turned *me* on—the power I felt, knowing my words enflamed him even more than the clips and the plug. That my words were enough to make him do these things.

"Yes, ma'am," he answered.

"Do you still have some lube left?"

"Yes, ma'am."

See? Smart boy, my Jack. Another man might have used it all up getting that butt plug properly situated. But Jack knew how to plan ahead. Some women might go for the dumb type, but not me. I respected intelligence, creativity. Turned me on.

I praised him accordingly.

"Now, Jack," I said, "I want you to open your pants and pull out your cock."

The way the webcam was pointed, I couldn't see his crotch, but I could tell from his upper-body motions what he was doing. Could tell by the look of relief on his face when his cock was free and in his hand.

"Are you fully hard?"

"Not yet, ma'am. Close."

"Use the lube, and bring yourself to full erection."

Oh, Jack's cock. My mouth watered at the thought of it. I'm not the type to think it's demeaning to go down on a man; I love the taste and feel of a velvet-and-steel rod in my mouth. Once at lunchtime I'd surprised him at work and hidden under his desk, licking and sucking him and keeping him on the edge for the full hour while he struggled to eat his Thai takeout and catch up on e-mail.

Hmm. I really was overdue to have him come to my work and hide under my desk and lick me until I came a few times. (After hours, of course, so no one would see his face glistening with my wetness. Then I'd send him off to a convenience store we never frequented to pick up something for me, my juices dried on his face but his skin smelling obviously of female musk.)

"I'm fully hard, ma'am."

"Good. Keep stroking yourself, but not enough to come yet."

I imagined his hand gripping his hard, slick length under the desk, sliding from balls to tip, with a little twist at the end to give the head extra stimulation. It was something I loved to watch, but I could imagine well enough.

My toes curled in my stockings. I wanted him. Soon.

"Ma'am!"

"Yes, Jack?"

He was frozen in place, eyes wide.

"I just saw my boss walk by. I…I need to stop."

Felicity Jordan, his new CEO. He'd admitted he was quite attracted to her. She was a sexy thing, to be sure: forty-five and mature, with a gym-strong body and wheat-colored hair cut in a thick bob.

"No," I said. "Keep going."

He broke protocol then, but I wouldn't hold it against him because he had a valid point. "We agreed this would never interfere with or jeopardize my job."

"And it won't, Jack. Keep going." I smiled again, a fresh wave of desire shivering through me as the game advanced. "I've made arrangements with Felicity. That would be Ms. Jordan to you tonight."

Confusion passed over his face, but to his credit, I could tell his arm was still moving, his fist was still stroking.

"She's made sure there's no one else there," I went on. "She also knows your safeword, and we've discussed your kinks. She's going to give you a spanking. When I get there, we'll both help you finish what we've started.

"Get up now and open your office door and let her in."

Jack stared at the webcam. Then, finally, he said, "Yes, ma'am," and disappeared from my view again.

I took another swallow of very fine Scotch. What I didn't tell him was that there was no need for me to drive there. I'd be watching the spanking from Felicity's own office, through her own webcam.

Then, in a little while, I'd just make my way down the hall and join them.

one thousand

THIS IS NOT a tale of revenge.

To a human, it might sound so, but I am only who I am. Just as a jeju striped field mouse cannot change its markings or a dhole cannot exist on grasses and berries, I cannot change how I am.

I am Kumiho, and what I do to men is just my nature.

*

You have heard many stories about me, no doubt, for my myth extends back to the beginning of time, before Korea was called as such. Nine fox-tails she has, they'll tell you, and that is true. That men cannot see my tails until it is to late is also fact.

That I am a seductress...well, why would that be a falsehood?

There are still things that the legends forget, that men forget to include in the tales.

They forget to ask "why?"

*

Night has slipped beyond the deep blue of twilight. The village is a small one, which means everyone was involved in the wedding festivities. Today, a sweet shy bride wed her handsome, slender groom. They feasted on rice cakes, sipped acacia wine (the groom indulged in some soju for added fortitude) before retiring to the bridal chamber.

It was a simple thing I did to cast a thrall across everyone, to send them to sleep. Even the anticipatory bride. Then to convince her groom to go to a different room, where he saw me in the visage of his bride. Where the candles didn't provide enough light for him to see the nine red-and black furred tails that flick behind me.

He saw me, and I saw the face and form of my own true love.

"Jin-Hwan," I murmured. I knew it wasn't truly him, but for all my heart I wished to believe it was, if only for this short night we had.

"Beloved," he said, reaching out to cup my face in his hand.

At the beginning of the world, there were gods, and there were the rest of us: spirits, demons, fey, there are many names. Then, the Kumiho was a fox spirit, sharing the sly qualities of the animal. A trickster, yes—capricious, even—but not malicious.

But then my betrothed, my beloved, whom I loved more than the breath of life itself, was killed. How it happened is no longer important, save that it was some game of the gods he stumbled into, and his life was inconsequential to them.

I raged, I ranted, I threw myself at the gods and denounced them, and they did what gods do: they cursed me.

Now, tonight, I spelled this man not only to believe I was his bride, but that it was months since their wedding night, that we were experienced together. I'd had enough of fumbling, enough of confused men wondering why his allegedly innocent bride acted with such abandon, knew such erotic tricks.

We kissed then, the feel of his lips against mine sending a thrill through me. It had been too long. I had missed him so much.

I arched against the length of his body. Smooth, sleek muscles against my slender curves. The yards of fabric that made up my wedding skirts were designed to hide my figure when I stood, but the red and blue silk was little barrier between us as we lay together.

Still, my clothing and his could have been made of wood or stone, for all they kept us apart. I sat up, swaying with heady desire, as Jin-Hwan untied my cheogori and slipped it off my shoulders.

He followed this with kisses along my newly bared flesh, sweet caresses up my arms, in the hollow of my throat, along the curve of my breasts, until I could have screamed with frustration. I moaned, encouraging him, and he became more bold, finally adding the scrape of teeth along my collarbone that I so craved.

Emboldened by my reaction, he fumbled with the long sashes that crossed above my breasts, anchoring my voluminous ch'ima to me. I hung, poised on the excruciating knife-edge decision of savoring the delicious delay or of giving in to frustration and helping him strip more away from between us.

Instead, I took the ends of the sashes from him, draped them across the back of his neck, pulled him closer to kiss him again. I took his lower lip between my teeth, tugged.

His gasp made the muscles in my stomach quiver.

I released my grasp to let him continue, urging him on with whispers and promises. Finally the knots released, and my small breasts were bared, free to his touch.

Jin-Hwan (because I believed it to be him, with all my will) sucked in his breath at the sight. I traced my fingers across my smooth stomach, up along my ribs, to frame my breasts. An invitation.

He needed no greater encouragement. He suckled my nipples, sending waves of pleasure through me. I grew wet between my thighs, dampening the crotch of my soggot, the final garment I wore. I shucked them off while he nipped at my tender skin.

If I couldn't control the bucking of my hips, shouldn't I put the movement to good use?

My fingers made quick work of the ties of his cheogori as well—after all, I had had centuries to practice. I could have, in fact, used magic to aid me, but these nights I preferred to savor each moment.

Yes, now! I could skim my hands across the smooth warm flesh of his chest.

Playfully I tweaked his nipples. He jerked against me, surprised and aroused. Oh, so aroused—his erection pressed long and hard against my thigh.

I curved my fingers around the length of him. The looseness of his paji allowed me to surround him in silk. Through the fabric, he burned hot. I stroked him. His hips jerked. Moisture seeped, darkening the silk.

"Beloved," he moaned.

Enough. I stripped his paji from him, drank in the sight of him, slender and proud. Inside I clenched in anticipation.

I surprised him by slipping out from beneath him, pressing him down so that I could straddle him. His dark eyes flashed with excitement.

I dipped forward to brush my mouth against his, promising, tasting. Pressing my lower lips against him, I coated him with my slickness.

Now I teased us both.

But no more. I raised up, let him slip inside of me.

I sank down. We both sighed, strangled noises in our throats.

Together, as one, finally.

I moved above him, sinuous as a viper, wicked as a fox, drawing out my own pleasure as I encouraged his. When the spasms overtook me, I keened, my womb and my heart clenching with a pleasure so intense it bordered on pain.

He was so close himself. Trembling with the effort to hold back, just a few brief moments more.

He believed he waited until my own pleasure was sated, and that was indeed greatly true, but I also used just a touch of my own magic to ensure what he intended.

I drew myself off of him, reluctantly and yet eagerly, for then I crouched between his slender thighs and he caught his breath again when he realized what I was about to do.

The sweet taste of our juices mingled on my tongue as I drew him into my mouth. Hands and tongue, lips and the barest hint of teeth, I brought him back to the edge.

My furred tails, of their own accord, undulated around me. When their softness flicked against his sac, tickling and caressing, he came.

And I drank.

He was helpless to control his spasms, which wracked his body longer than a normal orgasm would. He rode the waves of pleasure, unable to realize just how long the ecstasy lasted, and I rode them with him, shuddering again and again.

I could have killed him, of course. I could have drained the life essence completely from him, watched as his heart ceased to beat, leaving him an empty husk.

But that is not in my nature. That is my *choice*.

He slipped into unconsciousness, a final murmured "Beloved" caught on his lips.

They would find him in the morning, and curse my name even as they saw he lived. He would be too weak to marry that day; the wedding would be postponed. Sometimes the union was canceled altogether, with accusations that he was tainted from having slept with a demon. I hoped, as I always did, that this would not come to be.

I was not always so merciful. At first, I did take the men's lives. I couldn't control myself, but more than that, I was angry. My own love had been taken from me, taken on our wedding night, and this was the curse laid upon me.

I could not see him again until after death, and I could not die unless I were mortal.

I could not become mortal until I'd drunk the essences of one thousand men.

I lay in a puddle of silk atop the bamboo sleeping mat, breathing in the sweet scents of hibiscus and lovemaking. This should have been my wedding night. I regretted taking that away from the bride in the next room.

Pink dawn kissed the horizon, and my hold on the villagers weakened. I had to leave, had to be gone before the sun showed her face.

I rose, pressed a kiss to his forehead. My scattered garments vanished; I had no need of them.

With a final flick of my tails, I leapt from the windows.

One night in a thousand was gone. One night closer to my beloved Jin-Hwan.

santa claus is comin'

ARE YOU NAUGHTY or nice, little girl?

"Naughty" was the answer Jessica always came down on. Naughty, because she had a naughty, perverse, filthy little secret.

It had all started when she was a child, believing in magic and wonder and Santa Claus. The very first time she saw the Rankin-Bass special "Santa Claus is Comin' to Town," she'd been swept away. The woman in the animation was also named Jessica, so it was a short leap (just a hop and a skip, really) from there to little-girl Jessica imagining and pretending *she* was that Jessica.

Good, virtuous, animated Jessica helped rescue Kris Kringle so that he could bring toys to the children of Sombertown. She went on to marry him and become Mrs. Claus. And like little-girl Jessica, she yearned for a pretty porcelain doll to call her own.

When little-girl Jessica became young-adult Jessica, with all the attendant hormone overload, it had then been a short tumble into the gutter to imagining what Jessica and Kris did on their wedding night.

In specific, kinky detail.

Kris had this wide-eyed, pink-cheeked innocence to him, and that made the fantasies all the more depraved.

Now it was Christmas Eve once again, and Jessica had been sipping eggnog and wrapping presents and singing along with the animated special. (Oh, how she'd celebrated the day it was finally released on DVD!)

When Winter gave Kris the magic snow globe that allowed him to see who'd been naughty or nice, she shivered as she always did. Her clit pulsed even as her cheeks flushed. Naughty, always naughty.

Technically, Kris was quite the bad boy himself. He insisted on standing up to the Burgermeister Meisterburger and bringing toys to Sombertown when they were outlawed.

Jessica went for the bad boys, the rebels. Especially if they were redheads.

She set the final wrapped present under the tree, knocked back the last of the eggnog, and turned off all the lights except for the multicolored ones that blinked on the tree. Then she went to the bedroom to prepare for her final Christmas Eve ritual.

She shimmied into a scarlet satin peek-a-boo bra with the nipples cut out and matching crotchless panties, a short red velvet skirt trimmed with white faux fur, and thigh-high stockings striped red-and-white like candy canes. Jessica in the cartoon was always primly attired, but Jessica in real life knew about dressing for sex.

Adjusting the red-and-white velvet hat on her head, she settled back down on the living room sofa and closed her eyes.

"Naughty Jessica."

In her fantasies, he looked the same as he did in the animation: impossibly smooth skin, unusually large blue eyes, unearthly cartoon features. His motions weren't quite as smooth as they should be, but his shoulders were as broad as in the cartoon, something little kids probably never noticed.

"I *am* naughty," she purred, running her hands across her bare torso and over her bra. Her nipples had sprung to attention at his words, begging for his touch. "What are you going to do about it? Put coal in my stocking?"

His gaze dropped to her legs, his expression so shockingly lascivious that if he'd looked that way in the Rankin-Bass special, mothers everywhere would have been horrified—or gotten impossibly wet, just like Jessica was doing now.

"Seems to me," he said, "that your stocking are well filled. Guess I'll have to find some other way to punish you."

Jessica moaned, a fresh wave of desire pulsing through her.

He sat on a throne-like chair that had appeared in her living room like magic, just as he had. (Well, he'd come down the chimney, right? Like *that* wasn't phallic.) He patted his thighs. "Sit on Santa's lap."

On legs gone wobbly with lust, she obeyed. He drew her in for a bruising kiss, nipping at her lower lip until she gasped. Tweaking her nipples with his fingers, pinching hard enough to poise on the edge of pain, he said "What do you want for Christmas, hm?"

"You," Jessica managed, squirming on his lap. Beneath his red trousers, she felt his erection, and she wanted his cock inside her.

She knew she'd have to wait for the privilege, but it didn't stop her from asking.

"Well, let's see what Santa has in his sack for you." He picked up the bulging bag and began pulling out toys.

Her breath caught. Every year they were different. Maybe butt plugs and whips; maybe rabbit-fur mittens and tickly feathers.

This time he had clamps for her nipples, ones that ended with little green holiday bells. He always seemed to know how to accessorize the outfit she chose each year. She hissed against the pain as the teeth nipped into her sensitive flesh, and her cheeks flushed hot as the bells jingled merrily.

Red and gold ribbon, the kind you'd use to wrap a package, now wound between and over her wrists. He tied them together in a jaunty bow. Then he picked her up (this was magic and fantasy, after all) and arranged her over his lap, head down, ass up, his erection digging into her stomach.

He tugged her panties down just below the curve of her bottom, stripped off his gloves.

When she clenched her cheeks, he reached down and tugged on those vicious clamps, and she squealed.

"Hush now," he said. "Not a creature was stirring, not even a mouse."

She pressed her lips together and made no more sound than a whimper as he blistered her butt with his hand. Rosy cheeks, all part of the Santa milieu, but this wasn't what most people thought of. When his hand connected with her ass, it stung; when he paused, it throbbed. Throbbed in the same way her tortured nipples throbbed, throbbed in time with her wanting clit, her empty cunt.

One year he'd shown up with Topper the penguin, who'd stared at her with unblinking black eyes. Another year the Winter Warlock joined him, the two of them pushing her to her limits and beyond. Still, Kris was the only one she wanted. The only one she needed, craved.

He nudged her off his lap and stood. "Suck my cock," he said.

Dropping to her knees, Jessica unbuckled his wide shiny black belt and tugged town his red trousers. He sat back, sighing as she wrapped her still-bound hands around him.

His flesh felt smoother than a normal man's, cooler, unwrinkled. More like a dildo than a real penis. (She'd never seen him flaccid, so she didn't know how exactly that worked.) Under her hands and wet mouth, though, it grew warm, and a hard cock would feel incredible inside her no matter what it was made of.

She was already wet from the clamps and the spanking, even as she shifted from the discomfort of her heels rubbing into her stinging skin as she knelt before him. She would have loved to touch herself, release the ache between her thighs, but for now she concentrated on him, giving him the best head she could.

One year he'd given her a vibrator, watched her as he gave her instructions, making her come again and again until she thought she was too sensitive, then forcing her to come yet again.

Another year he'd fitted her with a bit and a butt plug with a brown-and-white tuft of a tail. He'd bent her over the arm of the throne, tugged on reins as he pounded into her, calling out the names of his reindeer.

Now, he finally helped her to her feet and led her to the sofa. Sitting down, he guided her onto his lap to straddle him. The scratchy wool of his half-pulled-down pants was like sandpaper on her ass when she sank all the way down on him.

The bells jingled merrily as she posted up and down on that smooth hard cock. Then she was grinding back and forth, only his hands on her waist keeping her from toppling off as she shuddered and moaned through her climax.

His own shout was jolly, the ho-ho-hos jerking from him in time to his final orgasmic thrusts.

*

Jessica awoke with a start, her neck aching from her uncomfortable splay on the sofa. In the blinking light, she saw that the cookies and eggnog she'd left out were gone.

Her inner thighs were sticky with pungent come, her ass tender and hot.

There was a new present under the tree, a box wrapped in blue paper with silver snowflakes printed on it, topped with a big silver bow. Jessica held with the tradition of opening one present on Christmas Eve, and that present was always the one from him.

With a tender smile, she lifted the porcelain doll from the box. She'd leave it under the tree for now; later, she'd put it into the case with all the others.

She unplugged the lights on the tree and headed upstairs to bed, weary and sated and already yearning for next Christmas Eve.

It wasn't sugarplums she'd be dreaming of…

the witch of venice

WE DON'T GET a lot of trick-or-treaters here in Venice Beach. The folks who live here are single, or use the tiny houses as cottages to get away from LA. Down by the beach, it's all college students and hippies. And I'd guess parents would worry about their little ghosts and fairies falling into the canals.

Still, Halloween's my favorite holiday, so I dress up just in case. As a witch, of course—only appropriate. A purple-and-black striped pointy hat with a big purple rose on it, and a black apron with purple bats scattered across it. Stripey tights, lace-up granny boots.

I stick little speakers in the windows and play eerie music on my iPod, and prop a small broom by the front door.

I get a few older kids, and give them slimy eyeball candies because they haven't bothered to dress up. A young couple comes by with an adorable little girl dressed as a cat, complete with drawn-on whiskers. She can't be more than three, and her pale blue eyes are wide when I open the door.

"What do you say?" her father prods her.

"Mm…pwease?"

I laugh and drop a couple of Starbursts into her plastic pumpkin. The mother thanks me before they retreat into the night.

I sit in my cracked cocoa-brown leather recliner and read *Amphigorey* and wait. The sketchy parade of children tapers off. Finally, there's another knock at the door.

Eva. Beautiful Eva.

She's more of a traditionalist—her outfit is all black. Her hat has a lace veil, and although her satin skirt reaches almost to the floor, it's skin tight, with a slit up the back. Her high-collared, buttoned-up top completes the Victorian look.

I think about unbuttoning those buttons, one at a time.

"Trick or treat," she says with a wicked smile, handing me a gift bag.

"Treat." I close the door, set the bag aside, and kiss her.

She's shorter than me, but wears higher heels, so we almost balance out. Still, I have to bend a little to find her raspberry lips, her dusky skin. She tastes like chocolate, not Snickers or Three Musketeers, but imported dark chocolate, rich and almost but not quite bitter. Adult chocolate.

Only after I've thoroughly kissed her, until we're both breathless and a little light-headed, do I peek into the bag. My thighs clench at what I see inside. "Minx," I say, and she just laughs.

I go to the bedroom and change. Not my whole outfit, just parts of it. I exchange the tights for fishnet thigh-highs, and the longer, flowing skirt for a short one, just barely longer than my apron. It's black, but I put a purple crinoline beneath it, which peeks naughtily out and makes the skirt flare.

My hands are shaking, and I'm already wet. Eva does that to me.

I dab on a little lip gloss and rejoin her in the living room. She has me twirl, to see my crinoline, and then she takes me by the hand and we exit into the magical night.

The canals are silent; the ducks asleep and no one out in their little boats. A few people are on their porches and we wave as we go by. They raise their glasses to us, calling out "Happy Halloween." I can't tell in the dim light whether they're someone who watched us last year, or the year before, on our annual trek.

At the edge of the ocean, we write on little pieces of paper something we want to give up this year, something we want to release from our lives. Then we light the scraps on fire and toss them into the waiting sea, which patiently takes them from us. We bury our toes in the sand, raise our hands to the sky, and give thanks both for the year past and the one to come, full of possibilities.

We run to the boardwalk, tie on our shoes, and hurry back to my little house as fast as we can go.

Not fast enough. Along a dark canal, Eva stops and pushes me up against the fence, kissing me hard. Her hands slide up under my skirt, cupping my ass, pulling my mound against her. I grind against her thigh, aching for her.

Laughing, she grabs my hand and we run again, to my street and onto my porch and then we tumble into the house.

I grab the iPod and speakers, and in the bedroom start the soundtrack to the Frank Langella version of *Dracula*.

My hands are sure now as I pluck at the column of tiny buttons on her blouse. It's a ritual in itself, this slow, careful process, slipping each black, faceted button through its hole, revealing another inch, a wider vee of skin. It's my legs that shake now, and my stomach quivers with the need that's building in me.

Her skirt slithers down to her ankles and she steps out of it. I bury my face between her breasts, breathing in patchouli, as I work on the buttons at her wrists. Finally she's there before me, naked except for a black thong and black high-heeled boots that lace all the way up her calves.

And her hat, of course. Crooked from our hasty passage, but still perched atop her glossy brown curls.

"Now you," she says, reaching for my clothes. My shirt shimmies over my head, followed by my bra. Eva steps back and grins. "I like the skirt," she says, and reaches under it again, this time to peel my panties away from my drenched lips. Her fingertips skid in my wetness, teasing around my clit, and I thrust forward. She pulls away, inhales the scent of my juices on my panties and her fingers, then tosses the underwear away.

Fingers, lips, tongues. We devour each other, hungry for plump nipples and salt-slick skin. As needy as I am, I can't wait to taste the best part of her. I kneel between her legs. She has tattoos on each of her jutting hipbones: a triskele on the left, a spiral on the right. At the small of her back, right before the swell of her cheeks, is a Goddess symbol, a full circle bordered by two crescent moons. I might see that later, but for now, I trace the two on her hips with my fingertips before parting her reddened lips and feasting.

You can't make me believe lovemaking isn't an act of devotion. I'm on my knees, worshiping at the altar of a veritable goddess. Would we be capable of such pleasure if the gods themselves didn't want us to be?

I slide my fingers into her, one, two, until my whole hand, tiny as it is, presses her open. Eva writhes and sobs and shudders and then cries out my name. An act of affirmation and life on a night that recognizes and honors death.

I snag the gift bag from the nightstand and toss the star-scattered sparkly tissue paper on the floor. I draw out Eva's present—my treat—a glorious purple dildo and matching harness.

I hold it up, cocking my head in a question, and she answers by reaching out for the items. "Tonight it's for me to wear and you to enjoy," she says.

I shiver as I watch her buckle the leather around her. I don't just want to feel that yummy fake cock inside me—I want to feel Eva wielding it, making it a part of her. So there's a frisson of disappointment when she lies on her back.

"Come here, baby," she says.

When I see her stroke the dildo lovingly with one hand, any regret I feel shivers away. Lying there with her tats visible between the leather straps, she *does* look like she owns the thing.

She looks glorious and wild and I want to feel her cock inside me. I straddle her in a rustle of crinoline and sink onto the fat silicone. We weave our fingers together. Rocking my hips, I let the dildo stretch me, fill me. The hair at the back of my neck stands up.

She pulls me down, tugs at my nipples with her teeth. The sweet pain lances down to my clit. I reach between us, beneath my flirty skirt to touch myself. I'm swollen and so on edge.

Eva pushes me back up. Hands on my hips, she grinds me back and forth, and I press my middle finger against my clit as the dildo rubs deep inside me.

"Sweet lady!" I gasp, and it doesn't matter whether I'm referring to Eva or something more abstract. We are all one, and I'm aware through the gripping star-shower of my orgasm that she's coming again, too.

At midnight, we go up onto the roof, where I've put out a mattress and a mound of pillows and zipped two sleeping bags together. We split open a pomegranate and feed each other the seeds, light candles for our ancestors, and sleep tangled together, waiting for the sun to rise on a new year.

*

How to Make the Witch of Venice Cocktail

> 1.5 oz vodka
> 0.5 oz Strega
> 1 oz orange juice
> 2 teaspoons crème de bananes

Fill a shaker halfway with ice cubes. Combine all ingredients in the shaker. Shake well. Strain into a cocktail glass, toast your ancestors, and enjoy!

your gift to me

THE SALESGIRL THINKS we're just friends. She probably wouldn't have let me accompany you into the dressing room if she knew we were lovers. They never let guys in, anyway, when I was dating them and brought them lingerie shopping with me. Then, I had to go into the stall by myself, and only if the rooms were in an enclosed area in the back of the store could I open the door and show him.

The salesgirl doesn't have to worry about much, really. I'm not going to touch you. You know it, and I know it. The wanting, the needing makes it even sexier.

You've never been one for fancy underthings. You've always been perfectly happy in your grey Jockey For Her separates. God knows I'd find you sexy in a sackcloth, so I never complained. But you knew, didn't you? You saw my wistful gaze when the Victoria's Secret catalogue arrived. I didn't mean to sigh aloud.

I know you've never felt your body was worth expensive, frothy scraps that revealed more than they showed. I hope our relationship has helped you with that. The mere fact that you're in this dressing room, with its pale pink walls and framed photos of models in bustiers and camisoles and semi-transparent robes trimmed with marabou, is a big step for you.

I give you a long, lingering kiss. You cling to me, just briefly, before I sit down in the ornately carved armchair with the fuchsia cushion in the corner.

You were a little overwhelmed when we got to the store. Too many choices. You paused just inside the door, blinking as if you'd just stepped into bright sunlight.

The salesgirl was a huge help. She had a good eye for what would best suit your coloring and body type. You've got a luscious hourglass figure: filmy camisoles and shortie chemises would just hang off you.

And, of course, technically it's *my* gift certificate. You put it in my Christmas stocking. Curled up together in front of the fire, mulled cider by our sides, we dove into our stockings with gusto, but you paused when you saw me open the embossed envelope.

You cleared your throat. "You get to pick the lingerie—for me. Whatever you want me to wear. Then we'll come home and…"

At that point, you just looked wicked. You might be shy about dressing up, but you're not shy in bed, not at all.

"And I'll unwrap my present," I finished. I couldn't wipe the grin off my face, or stop the frisson of arousal that pooled between my legs.

I thanked you and kissed you, and you kissed me back, and we knocked over our cider when we ripped each other's clothes off, but we didn't care.

You turn away from me know, hesitating before picking up the first outfit. I'm not surprised you picked the plainest of the offerings first: A bra-and-panty set in royal blue satin.

When you turn around, I can see the outline of your erect nipples, no fancy lace or pattern to hide their obvious, proud need. Hell, I can even see the crinkle of your pubic hair through the smooth fabric below.

I shift restlessly in the chair. It's getting warm in here. If you're getting as aroused as I am already—and it seems you are, giving the state of your nipples—we might have to buy every panty you try on.

You move on to more sets. A deep burgundy set catches my eye—it's elegant, not flashy. Lace overlays the silk beneath. There's a tiny single drop pearl at the center, between the breasts, and a scattering of pearls in a flower pattern at the front of the panties. A set to be worn for showing off, not for every day.

I can see you like the boy shorts, even the stretch lace ones. I figured you would, just as I figured the thongs would make you uncomfortable. Too exposed, too different from what you're used to. That's okay. Ditto the black bodystocking—a bit much, this time. Maybe later.

The emerald green satin teddy looks good on you, especially with that little ruffle at the edges. I enjoy watching you shimmy into it, adjust the straps. You're getting more comfortable, and I'm just getting more aroused. At this rate, I'm going to have to buy a fresh pair of panties myself.

I can't help it. I get up, pull you into my arms. My fingers skim up and down your back, enjoying the feel of the slick satin. You grab me, holding on tight, channeling all your nervousness into the kiss.

Nervousness, and excitement as well. My leg insinuates itself between yours, and I can feel the heat from your crotch. Thrilled, I nip at your lower lip, and you moan, long and low.

The salesgirl chooses that moment to knock on the door and ask how we're doing. You look horrified at first, but I merrily sing out that we're fine, just having trouble deciding, and she goes away. You and I break down in giggles.

In the end, my choice is clear. I pick the garnet-red merry widow, with matching stockings and a ribbon to tie around your neck. I saw your face change when you looked in the mirror. You saw how it displayed your breasts, how the lacy panties teased your ass, rising up just high enough to reveal the lower curve of your cheeks.

I pick this because you feel beautiful in it.

The fact that I want to press my lips to the pouting sliver of flesh that the panties highlight above your thighs is just an added bonus.

(When you're not looking, I give the salesgirl the royal blue satin bra-and-panties set, and a few of the stretch lace boy shorts, to ring up as well.)

"Do you want to grab something to eat?" I ask as we leave the store, figuring this would give you time to relax a little.

But you cuddle up close next to me, clutching the fancy bag containing our purchases, and whisper, "No. I want to go home and model for you."

The eagerness in your voice nearly makes me come right there.

When we get home, you banish me to the kitchen to pour us each a glass of Chardonnay while you get ready. My hand are shaking; it's hard to cut the foil, much less get the corkscrew in straight. Thankfully I'm not actually holding the full glasses when I hear you softly say my name.

I turn. You're in the doorway, wearing that incredible confection. Bouncing just a little on your toes, as if you can't stand still.

To hell with the wine.

I lead you to the standing mirror in the corner of our bedroom. It's an antique, one of the first things we bought together, polished mahogany wood and turned posts. You duck your head, but I gently encourage you to look at yourself. To see what I see.

"You look stunning in this," I tell you. "And you know it, too. See how it hugs your beautiful, curvy figure. Look how your breasts are just begging to be worshipped."

I stand close behind you, cup your breasts in my hands. I stroke the lace over your nipples with my thumbs. The buds are barely visible, almost the same color as the fabric, but I find them easily because they're tight and hard with excitement.

You gasp and press back against me.

"See how wonderful lace is?" I say. "How good it feels when it rasps across your sensitive nipples?"

I glide my hands down your waist, along your hips, murmuring endearments as I go. Then, I just can't hold back any longer. I move one hand forward, dip into the panties.

You're drenched.

Your eyes flutter shut as I find your clit and start to stroke.

"No, keep them open."

You try. You try so hard, but in the end, you can't. You can't even stand up anymore, so it's onto the bed with us. I lie next to you and kiss you and keep sliding my fingers across your clit until your thighs tremble and your pussy pulses and you explode. I keep my hand there, feeling your shuddering subside.

You reciprocate, lips and hands, teasing my nipples, kissing your way down my stomach. Then your fingers are inside me while you use your tongue to flick at me, and just before

I come I look down and see you kneeling there, your curvy bottom in the air, and I have to fantasize again about those brilliant red lace panties because I forgot to play with them before, and then I can't think straight at all.

Later—much later—you see me smiling, and tease me gently, tracing the outline of my lips with your forefinger. You think I'm smiling because I'm happy, because I enjoyed this so much, because I'm sated.

You're mostly right.

What you don't know is that for Valentine's Day, I'm getting you a gift certificate to that sex shop over on Division Street. You can pick out any toys you like.

And that night, you can use them all on me.

tie me up

TIE ME UP. Please.

I know you like it when I beg.

Tie me up. It's the only way I can feel free, only way I can let go. Shiny clanking handcuffs, smooth ropes, silk scarves, red leather fur-lined restraints, your red-dotted Burberry tie.

I want it. I need it. I crave it.

And then there's you. You need it, too, don't you? You need to see me relax into my bonds, accept the place you've let me escape to.

When my eyes close for the blindfold, you brush a soft kiss on my lips and whisper, "I love you."

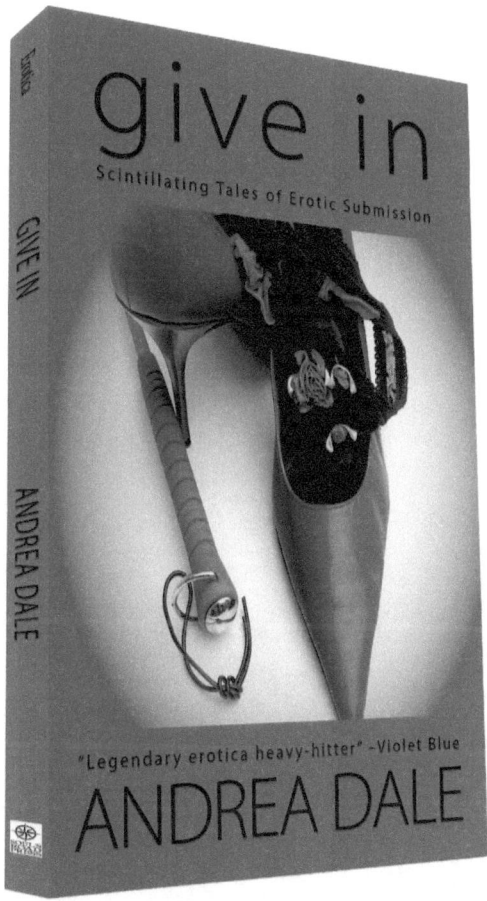

Naughty in Nature
Sizzling Stories of Sex in the Great Outdoors

Available in print and ebook
at all your favorite retailers!

about the author

Called a "legendary erotica heavy-hitter" (by the über-legendary Violet Blue), Andrea Dale writes sizzling erotica with a generous dash of romance. Her work—which has been called "poignantly erotic," "heartbreaking," and "exceptional"—has appeared in fourteen year's best volumes as well as about a hundred other anthologies from Soul's Road Press, Harlequin Spice, and Cleis Press, including her recent novella, *Kiss on Her List*.

She finds passion in rock music, clever words, piercing blue eyes, the wind in her hair, and the scent of the ocean.

Visit AndreaDaleAuthor.com for more information.

"Lie Back" (as "Fond Memories") originally appeared at
Hoot Island's Flash Contest, June 2002

"Undoing the Laces" originally appeared in *Hide and Seek*,
Cleis Press, 2007

"The Heist" originally appeared in *Frenzy: 60 Stories of Sudden Sex*,
Cleis Press, 2008, and was reprinted in The Mammoth Book of
Quick & Dirty Erotica, Running Press, 2013

"The Last Rays of the Summer Sun" originally appeared in
Best Lesbian Romance 2013, Cleis Press, 2013

"A Healthy Dose" originally appeared in *The Big Book of
Domination*, Cleis Press, December 2014

"A Sensitive Sole" originally appeared in *The Sexiest Soles: Erotic
Stories About Feet and Shoes*, Alyson Books, 2006

"Water" originally appeared at ForTheGirls.com, 2004.

"Peppermint Stick" originally appeared at Torquere Press, 2004,
and was expanded and republished as part of Circlet Press's 2008
online Erotic Advent Calendar

"After the Rain" originally appeared in *Travelrotica for Lesbians:
Erotic Travel Adventures*, Alyson Books, August 2006

"Bathing Beauty" originally appeared in
Rubber Sex, Cleis Press, 2008

"Taming His Wild Cat" originally appeared in
Sudden Sex: 69 Sultry Short Stories, Cleis Press, 2013

"Come As You Are" originally appeared in
Sudden Sex: 69 Sultry Short Stories, Cleis Press, 2013

"Devouring Heart" originally appeared in
The Sweetest Kiss: Ravishing Vampire Erotica, Cleis Press, 2009

"From Bitter to Sweet" originally appeared in *Got a Minute?
60 Second Erotica* (Cleis Press, 2007)

"Guess Who's Coming to Dinner" originally appeared at
ForTheGirls.com, August 2006.